Guess Who's Here?

Emily had just sat down at the lunch table when Marie Webster came over to her. "Emily, your family is out front," Marie told her. "They need help taking something out of the car. I understand it has something to do with a surprise they brought for you. Why don't you see if you can lend a hand?"

Emily dashed out of the dining room and through the hall to the front door. As she bounded out onto the porch, she saw her mother, her father, and Eric. Eric was helping somebody out of the backseat. Emily's eyes widened in disbelief and joy as she saw one slim leg emerge, then another encased in a plaster cast. A hand thrust out a pair of crutches, which Eric took, and then a petite blond girl, her hair in two ponytails, hopped out, grabbing the crutches from Eric.

"*Judy?*" Emily shouted, immediately recognizing her best friend. "Judy, is it really you?"

Judy grinned, tucking the crutches under both arms. "I—————ll right!"

Emily ——————————————— e it to
Webste——————————

Other books in the **HORSE CRAZY** series:

SURPRISE, SURPRISE!
by Virginia Vail

Illustrated by Daniel Bodé

Troll Associates

Library of Congress Cataloging-in-Publication Data

Vail, Virginia.
    Surprise, surprise! / by Virginia Vail; illustrated by Daniel
Bode.
    p.   cm.—(Horse crazy ; #4)
    Summary: When her best friend Judy comes to visit the riding camp
where thirteen-year-old Emily is spending the summer, Judy is a big
hit with the other campers and Emily suddenly feels left out and
jealous.
    ISBN 0-8167-1657-9 (lib. bdg.)   ISBN 0-8167-1658-7 (pbk.)
    [1. Camps—Fiction.   2. Friendship—Fiction.   3. Horses—Fiction.]
I. Bode, Daniel, ill.   II. Title.   III. Series: Vail, Virginia.
Horse crazy ; #4.
PZ7.V192Su   1990
[Fic]—dc19   89-31346

A TROLL BOOK, published by Troll Associates,
Mahwah, NJ 07430

Copyright © 1990 by Troll Associates, Mahwah, New Jersey

Printed in the United States of America.

10   9   8   7   6   5   4   3   2   1

Chapter One

"Look out below!"

Emily Jordan, floating happily on her back in the crystal-clear pool just below Willoughby Falls, gave a squawk and backstroked as fast as she could to get out of the way of the small, red-haired cannonball hurtling her way. She climbed out of the water just as Libby Dexter dropped in with a huge splash and surfaced a second later, grinning.

"My *hair*! You got my hair all *wet*!" wailed Caro Lescaux, blinking water out of her eyes. "Libby, you're a menace! *Must* you play Tarzan all the time? Or maybe I should say, Cheetah!"

Making cheerful monkey noises, Libby swam to the rocks that bordered the pool and clambered out, making for the rope that swung from a sturdy branch overhead.

"My turn next," Danny Franciscus called out. She caught the rope in both hands, got a running start, and sailed out over the water, letting go and landing with an even bigger splash.

"Really!" Caro said crossly. "What's the matter with you two, anyway? You act like you're four years old instead of fourteen. Now my hair is positively *drenched*!"

"In the first place," Libby shouted as she swung back and forth on the rope, "I'm a mere child of thirteen, for your information. And in the second place, who cares if your hair is wet? So's everybody else's. Join the club!" She let out a long howl, then yelled, "Geronimo!" and hit the water just as Caro hastily climbed out. "Hey, Emily, want to take a turn?" Libby asked, paddling over to where Emily was now perched on a big rock.

"Nope. The last time I did it, I got water up my nose," Emily said. "Besides, I'm starting to get pruney. I think I'll dry off in the sun."

Libby scrambled up beside her, shaking her short, wet hair like a little dog, and Danny climbed out, too. Emily noticed that Libby's lips had turned an interesting shade of purple, and she was shivering. No wonder—she'd been in the water ever since they had arrived at the Falls over an hour ago. But Danny didn't look cold at all as she squeezed the water out of her long, dark braid.

Danny lay back on the sun-warmed rock, folding her arms behind her head. "Boy, isn't this terrific?" she sighed. "I'm so glad Pam decided to

2

take us on this overnight trail ride. I was beginning to think we'd never get to go at all."

"Me, too," Libby said. "Pam's the best counselor at Webster's. And it sure was a bummer when we got rained out the first time, and Dru fell off her horse and refused to budge an inch."

Emily looked over to where Dru Carpenter was sitting in the shade of a tree with Penny Marshall and Lynda Graves. Dru, Penny, Lynda, Libby, Danny, Caro, and Emily were all Fillies, the twelve-to-fourteen-year-olds at Webster's Country Horse Camp. Penny was showing Dru how to make a daisy chain with some black-eyed Susans she'd picked earlier, and Dru was singing along with the music on Lynda's portable tape player.

"Dru sure has changed a lot since then," Emily said. "She's not scared of horses anymore, and she's not nearly as shy as she used to be." She grinned. "Come to think of it, *I'm* not as shy anymore, either."

"You? *Shy?*" Danny said, raising her head to stare at her. "Come on, Emily. Get serious!"

"Well, I was at first. I was afraid I'd be lonely and homesick and I wouldn't make any friends. But now I've been at Webster's almost four weeks, I feel as if I've known you and the rest of the Fillies forever."

Libby turned her head to look at Caro, who was sitting on the trunk of a fallen tree, scowling and combing her long golden hair. "I know what you mean," she said. "And in at least one case, it seems like *more* than forever!"

3

Emily giggled. "Yeah. Caro's kind of hard to take sometimes. But I really think she's getting better."

"Better?" Libby repeated thoughtfully. "Yeah, I guess maybe you're right. Better than chicken pox, or deerflies, or poison ivy, or—"

The girls muffled snorts of laughter, and Caro glanced in their direction, perfect brows arched questioningly. Then she shrugged and returned to her hair.

"Uh . . . Libby, speaking of poison ivy, you see those shiny green leaves all over that log Caro's sitting on?" Danny asked. "I can't really tell from here, but don't they kind of look like . . . "

Libby propped herself up on her elbows and looked. Then she turned to Emily and nodded very solemnly. "Think we ought to tell her?"

"Libby! Of course we should tell her," Emily said, trying hard not to grin.

"Oh, all right." Libby sat up and called, "Hey, Caro, do you know you're sitting in a clump of poison ivy?"

The pretty blond girl looked over at her and shook her head, smiling smugly. "Oh, right. Sure I am. Honestly, Libby, I bet you go around telling people their shoes are untied on April Fool's Day."

"Only if they are," Libby said.

Caro kept on French-braiding her hair. "How dumb do you think I am, anyway?" she said with a smirk.

4

Libby and Emily looked at each other. "Your turn," Libby said.

Emily sighed. "Caro, remember that chart in the camp store? The one with the pictures of poisonous plants? Remember what poison ivy looks like?"

"Of course I do," Caro snapped. "Three shiny green leaves on a single stem, with reddish veins . . . ." She stared down at the greenery around her. "Holy cow, it *is* poison ivy!" She jumped up. "Poison ivy! I've been sitting in *poison ivy*! Somebody *help*! Why didn't anybody *tell* me?"

Emily and Libby looked at each other again and shrugged. Danny giggled.

"Calm down, Caro." Pam Webster, the Fillies' counselor, climbed out of the water, where she had been enjoying a peaceful, solitary swim, and slung a towel around her shoulders. She strode over to the pile of camping gear that had not yet been unpacked, pulled out a duffel bag, and rummaged through it until she found the first-aid kit. Caro danced frantically around her, scratching at the backs of her thighs and calves, crying, "Hurry! Oh, Pam, hurry up!"

Pam calmly took out a plastic bottle and handed it to her. "It couldn't possibly have started itching yet. You just think it does. Here, this is green soap. Take a washcloth, pour on plenty of soap, and scrub everywhere the leaves may have touched your skin. It'll remove the oils, and you probably won't itch at all."

Caro snatched a facecloth from the duffel bag,

5

then opened the cap of the bottle and sniffed. "Yuck! This smells like the soap in the washroom at school," she said, wrinkling her nose.

"That's exactly what it is," Pam told her. "Would you rather itch or smell?"

"Ohhh!" Caro groaned, flouncing over to the pool and beginning to scrub.

"You just can't tell some people anything," Libby said cheerfully. She stood up and stretched. "I'm going to go say hello to Foxy. You guys want to come along?"

"Oh, yes," Emily said, jumping to her feet. "I haven't paid Joker a visit since we got here."

"You two go ahead," Danny said. "I'm going to take off this wet bathing suit. It's starting to feel clammy."

They slipped their bare feet into their sneakers and climbed down off the rock. Danny waved and headed toward the tree where she'd left her backpack.

"I hope the deerflies and mosquitoes aren't eating Joker alive," Emily worried.

"I hope they won't eat *us* alive," Libby said, glancing over at the horses who were tethered under the trees. "Got any of that insect-repellent spray?"

"We do," said Lynda, tossing her an aerosol can. "This stuff really works. We all sprayed each other when we got out of the water, and we haven't been bitten at all."

"We sprayed our horses, too," Dru added.

"Donna has very sensitive skin. I'd hate for some nasty bug to take a bite out of her."

Libby sprayed Emily, then Emily sprayed Libby before they went further into the woods, paying special attention to their ankles and shins to avoid a tick attack. As they approached, all the horses raised their heads and pricked their ears forward, glad of human company. Joker tossed his head and whickered softly as he always did whenever he hadn't seen Emily for a while, and Emily's heart beat faster as it always did when she hadn't seen Joker for a while. The big palomino was the most beautiful, most intelligent, most completely wonderful horse she had ever seen in her whole life. She still couldn't quite believe her luck at having him assigned to her for the summer. Joker was a dream come true—Emily had always wanted a horse of her own, and for these six weeks at Webster's Country Horse Camp, Joker was all hers.

Now his sleek golden coat was dappled with flecks of late-afternoon sunlight that filtered through the branches of the trees, and Emily thought he looked more beautiful than ever. She put her arms around his neck and pressed her cheek against him, murmuring a loving greeting. She was glad it was cool here in the shade. There didn't seem to be too many flies or mosquitoes around, either. Nevertheless, she took the spray can from Libby and misted her horse all over, then gave it back to Libby so she could do the same for Foxy, her reddish bay gelding.

7

It had been a long ride to Willoughby Falls, and Pam Webster, the daughter of Matt and Marie Webster who owned and ran the camp, had led the way. Her younger brother, Chris, brought up the rear with the pack horse that carried everything the campers couldn't fit into the blanket rolls tied behind their horses' saddles. Soon they would set up their tents, and Chris would start the fire so they could cook hamburgers and hot dogs. Emily was thrilled. Although she had gone camping with her parents once or twice, she'd never been on an overnight trail ride, and everything she did with Joker was more special than anything she'd ever done before.

"I wish Judy could be here, too," she told Joker, rubbing him behind the ears. "I've told her all about you in my letters, and I sent her a snapshot, but it's not the same as actually *seeing* you."

Judy Bradford, Emily's very best friend, was supposed to come to Webster's with her, but she'd broken her leg, so Emily had come alone. To make up for Judy's missing the wonderful summer they'd been looking forward to for so long, Emily wrote to her almost every day, keeping her up to date on all the exciting things Emily and the rest of the Fillies were doing. Mostly she wrote about Joker, and in her last letter, Emily had told her about Field Day, when Webster's girls competed against Long Branch, the boys' camp across the Winnepac River, in riding and other sports. Emily and Joker had won second prize in the intermediate horsemanship class, and best of all, they had been awarded the grand prize for best costume in the Costume Parade. That was two days ago, and Emily was still basking in a glow of pride.

"Hey, Emily. Look!" Libby cried.

Emily looked, and saw her friend standing barefoot on Foxy's back, arms extended.

Emily gasped. "Libby, be careful! You'll fall!" she exclaimed.

"Who, me? No way," Libby said, grinning. "Don't forget, my grandmother used to be a bareback rider in the circus."

How could Emily possibly forget? Libby's Gram had arrived at Webster's last week just when it looked as if Field Day was going to be a total disaster. None of the costumes were ready, and the girls on the softball team couldn't throw or hit the ball! Somehow, from the moment the feisty little woman with the twinkling blue eyes appeared in the activity room where all the campers were struggling to make their costumes, things began to get better. Emily privately thought of Libby's Gram as the camp's "fairy grandmother" because she'd not only been able to take Caro down a peg or two (as Gram would have said), but she'd also made peace between the Fillies and the Thoros, the oldest campers, when it looked as if the two groups would never speak to each other again.

"Libby, what's the matter with you? You nuts or something?"

Chris Webster had come over to check on his

roan gelding, Buster, and his little pinto pack horse, Splotch. He treated Libby as if she were a flaky younger sister. They'd known each other for years, because Libby had been coming to Webster's for a long time. Emily liked Chris a lot. He reminded her of her brother Eric, though Chris was blond and Eric was dark, and Chris, fourteen, was a year younger than Eric. But they both had a friendly, cheerful manner, and neither one was the least bit conceited, unlike Chris's older brother, Warren, who also helped out at Webster's.

Libby rolled her eyes and slid down to a sitting position. "No, I am *not* nuts. I was just fooling around." She swung one leg over Foxy's neck and slipped to the ground. "You going to start the campfire soon? I'm really starved! I can almost taste those hot dogs now."

"You're not going to taste anything if you don't come help with the tents and the food," Chris said. "You, too, Emily. I guess Joker will live without you for an hour or two till you bring him his supper."

Emily laughed. Chris knew how she felt about Joker, and because he was just as horse crazy as she was, he understood. "We're coming, slave driver," she said, as Libby shoved her feet back into her sneakers.

Chris pretended to be insulted. "Slave driver? Me? Hey, since I'm the only guy on this trip, I have to throw my weight around or all you girls would gang up on me! C'mon, let's go."

10

*　　*　　*

Twilight was drifting into darkness by the time the Fillies, Pam, and Chris had set up the tents, fed their horses, and polished off the entire supply of hamburgers, hot dogs, ice-cold lemonade, and the butterscotch brownies that Marie Webster had baked for dessert. Now they sat on blankets around the campfire, toasting marshmallows and not saying much—just enjoying the fresh, cool mountain air and gazing up at the moon that floated overhead in the darkening sky. It was almost full, Emily noticed drowsily; it had been only a sliver when she'd first arrived at Webster's. She and Libby were seated back to back, leaning against each other for support. The only sounds other than the campers' voices were the chirping of crickets, the droning of cicadas, and the roar of the waterfall, punctuated by the occasional hoot of an owl. Nice, Emily thought. Very nice.

"How about a song, Chris?" Pam asked, popping a marshmallow into her mouth.

Chris, who had brought along his guitar, strummed a chord or two. "Anything in particular?" he asked.

"How about 'Oh! Susannah'?" suggested Lynda.

"Too bouncy," Danny mumbled.

" 'My Bonnie Lies Over the Ocean'?" Penny said.

"Okay. Here goes . . . . " Chris changed into another key, and everyone began to sing:

12

"My Bonnie lies over the ocean,
My Bonnie lies over the sea,
My Bonnie lies over the ocean,
Oh, bring back my Bonnie to me.
Bring back, bring back,
Oh, bring back my Bonnie to me, to me.
Bring back, bring back,
Oh, bring back my Bonnie to me . . . . "

They sang the whole song, but Emily didn't hear the last verse. By then she was fast asleep.

Chapter Two

The next morning, after a breakfast of Marie's home-baked apple–raisin-bran muffins, hard-boiled eggs, apple juice, and fruit, everyone struck their tents, saddled their horses, and strapped their blanket rolls behind their saddles, preparing for the trip back to camp. Libby, Lynda, Pam, and Chris had taken an early swim, but Emily and the other Fillies just washed up and brushed their teeth. Emily thought the mountain air was far too chilly for a plunge into the icy water. She wished they could stay longer at Willoughby Falls, but on the other hand, she didn't want to miss riding class that afternoon. Usually riding instruction was held in the morning, but because of the trail ride, Matt Webster had scheduled it after lunch and water sports.

"Boy, were you ever out of it last night!" Libby

14

said as she sprang into Foxy's saddle. "I bet you don't even remember me dragging you into the tent when campfire was over."

"You're right," Emily admitted. "I was really zonked. When I woke up this morning, for a minute I didn't know where I was." She mounted Joker and gathered up the reins, falling in line behind Libby as they joined the others.

Caro, on her big bay gelding, Dark Victory, trotted past them and waved. As usual, she looked as if she'd just stepped out of the pages of a fashion magazine. Every blond hair was in place, and unlike the rest of the campers, who were wearing jeans and sweatshirts in addition to the hard riding hats that everyone at Webster's wore whenever they were on horseback, she had on stretch pants that fit her like a glove, and a designer polo shirt. How did she do it? Emily wondered. The polo shirt wasn't even slightly wrinkled, though it had been jammed into her blanket roll just like everybody else's clothes.

"How's the poison ivy, Caro?" Libby said.

"Not a single itch, thank you very much," Caro called over her shoulder. "That green soap really did the trick."

Libby sighed. "Too bad!" she whispered to Emily.

"Libby, you're terrible." Emily giggled.

"I am, aren't I?" Libby agreed cheerfully.

They arrived at Webster's shortly before noon, just in time for lunch. Emily realized that she was absolutely starving. But before she headed for the farmhouse dining room, she made sure that Joker was cool, dry, watered, and fed. Then she decided to stop by the Fillies' cabin to see if there was any mail for her. There was. A letter from her mother said that she, Emily's father, and Eric would be arriving at Webster's some time on Wednesday. They'd spend the night at a motel in Winnepac, then go on to Saratoga for a few days and return to the camp in time for the dressage exhibition on Sunday. *And* they were bringing Emily a big surprise.

Wednesday? That was today! Emily was delighted. If they arrived in time, they might even be able to watch her riding lesson. What could the surprise be? A box of fudge? A new pair of riding pants? The best surprise was that they were actually coming. They'd planned on attending Field Day, but Emily's father had a last minute business trip. She could hardly wait to show them the ribbons she'd won.

Emily tucked the letter under her pillow and made tracks for the farmhouse. She'd hardly had time to sit down next to Libby at the Fillies' table and sink her teeth into a tuna sandwich when Marie came over to her and said, "Emily, your folks are here. Think there's room for them at your table?" Marie was wearing a white chef's apron over her blue jean cutoffs and T-shirt, and her short blond hair was almost completely concealed by the blue bandanna she'd tied around her head. And, as usual, she was smiling. Emily thought Marie had the nicest smile she'd ever seen.

"They are? They're here already?" Emily leaped to her feet. "Terrific!"

"They're out in front," Marie told her. "Warren is helping them take something out of the car. I understand it's something to do with the surprise they brought for you."

A really *big* box of fudge? Or maybe they'd decided to bring one of those huge metal cannisters of pretzels they knew Emily loved dearly—the ones that could break every tooth in your head if you weren't careful.

"Why don't you see if you can lend a hand?" Marie suggested, her eyes sparkling. "I think this is the kind of surprise you're going to like very much."

Emily dashed out of the dining room and through the hall to the front door. As she bounded out onto the porch, she saw her mother, her father, and Eric. Eric was helping somebody out of the back seat. Emily's eyes widened in disbelief and joy as she saw one slim leg emerge, then another encased in a plaster cast. A hand thrust out a pair of crutches, which Eric took, and then a petite blond girl, her hair in two ponytails, hopped out, grabbing the crutches from Eric.

"*Judy?*" Emily shouted. "Judy, is it really you?"

Judy grinned, tucking the crutches under both arms. "Better believe it, Emily! It's me, all right!"

With a whoop, Emily raced across the porch and threw her arms around her very best friend.

"Wow! This *is* a surprise!" she cried. "I never thought—I mean, Mom didn't say—hey, Judy, welcome to Webster's!"

"Nice to see you, too, Emily," her father said, beaming at her.

"Daddy!" Emily turned to him and gave him a big hug. "Mom!" Another hug for her mother.

"How're you doing, sis?" Eric said.

Emily flung her arms around him next. "I just can't *believe* this!" she exclaimed happily. "All my favorite people right here at Webster's, my favorite place!"

Judy laughed. "We said we were going to horse camp together, didn't we? So when your folks told me they were coming up to see you and asked if I'd like to go along, I said yes. My parents said I could go, so here I am. It's not exactly the way we planned, but it's better than nothing, right?"

"Is it ever!" Emily said. "How's your leg feeling? Does it hurt or anything? Should you be sitting down?"

"Not yet," Judy said. "And no, it doesn't hurt a bit. I just get tired sometimes. But I brought my Rolls Royce," she said, gesturing at the wheelchair Eric had just unloaded from the trunk of the car, "so when I do, you can push me around."

"Hey, I've always wanted to push you around!" Emily teased.

"Emily, honey, you look so . . . so different, somehow," her mother said, coming up to Emily and brushing a wisp of brown, wavy hair off her forehead. "Your hair has grown, and I believe *you*

19

have, too. And you're so tanned! Doesn't she look wonderful, Frank?"

"She does indeed," Mr. Jordan agreed. "Obviously, all this fresh air, exercise, and sunshine agrees with her."

"I bet they feed you pretty well here, too," Eric added. "And speaking of food, Mrs. Webster said something about lunch. I don't want to break up this happy family reunion, but I'm pretty hungry."

"Me, too," Judy said. "I'm *always* hungry lately. What with eating so much and not being able to move around a lot, I'll probably be the size of the Goodyear blimp by the end of the summer!"

"Oh, sure!" Emily scoffed, eyeing her petite friend up and down. "That'll be the day. Come on, everybody. Marie said you could all sit with the Fillies, and they're dying to meet you." She turned to her friend. "Judy, you want the wheelchair?"

Judy shook her head. "No way. I can manage fine on my crutches. Let's go!"

Emily led the way to the dining room, giving her family and Judy a brief guided tour as she did.

"That's the camp store," she said, pointing to a room on their left as they entered the farmhouse. "And down that hall is the living room where we can watch TV or videos. That door over there is Matt's office—you should see all the trophies and ribbons he won when he was riding jumpers in the big horse shows! The Websters live upstairs. It's private, so none of us go there unless we're invited. And the kitchen's over there, and the laundry's in the basement, and this," she announced, pausing in the doorway to the dining room, "is where we eat. Like it said in the brochure, we all help Marie in the kitchen, and we help out in the vegetable garden and pick stuff for our meals." She paused for breath, very much aware that the eyes of all the campers, from the youngest Foal to the oldest Thoro, were focused on her, her parents, Eric, and Judy. Instead of feeling shy at being the center of attention, Emily was proud and happy to show off her pretty mother, her handsome father and brother, and her very best friend in the whole world.

Matt Webster stood up from his place at the Foals' table and came over to them, shaking hands all around.

"Your daughter is becoming an accomplished rider," he told Mr. and Mrs. Jordan. Turning to Eric, he asked, "Are you horse crazy, too, like your sister?"

Eric grinned. " 'Fraid not. I like engines—cars, motorcycles, stuff like that."

Matt nodded pleasantly, then turned and smiled at Judy. "Glad to meet you at last, Judy Bradford. Emily has told us so much about you. Too bad you couldn't be here for the whole summer, but at least you can stay with us for the rest of the week in the Fillies' cabin. I bet Emily's excited about that," he added, winking at Judy.

Emily's eyes widened. "She is?" She stared at Judy. "You are?"

Judy nodded vigorously. "That's another surprise. While your folks and Eric go to Saratoga, the Websters said I could bunk with you guys till your family gets back on Sunday for the dressage exhibition."

"Fantastic!" Emily crowed. "You can have the bunk over Caro's—no, that won't work out. You can't climb up the ladder. Well, Caro will just have to switch. I'm sure she won't mind—*too* much."

"Oh yes, she will," Judy said with a giggle. "If she's anything like you've told me in your letters, she's going to mind a *lot*!"

Emily giggled, too. "You've got a point there. Well, we'll worry about that later. Right now, I want you to meet everybody." She led her family and Judy over to the Fillies' table. "Guess what, gang?" she said happily. "Remember me telling you about my friend Judy who was supposed to come with me to camp? Well, she's here! And this is my mom, my dad, and my brother, Eric." She made introductions all around.

Mrs. Jordan smiled at the Fillies and at Pam. "I feel I know you all already. Emily's written so much about you."

"She sure has," Judy chimed in. "And she's sent pictures, too. I would have known who you were even if she hadn't just told us your names."

"Judy's going to stay in our cabin while my folks and Eric go to Saratoga for a few days," Emily said.

"Hey, cool!" Libby exclaimed. "She can have

the bunk over Caro's—the one Gram slept in. Oops! No, I guess you can't," she said to Judy. "Not with your leg in a cast."

"Of course she can't," Caro said. Emily and Judy glanced at each other, and Judy made an "I told you so" face. But to their amazement, Caro went on to say, "She can have my bunk. I don't mind taking the upper for a while. After all, any friend of Emily's is a friend of mine."

Emily couldn't have been more surprised if Caro had started turning cartwheels in the middle of the table. But when she saw the way Caro was looking at Eric, she understood perfectly.

"Please sit down and have some lunch," Pam offered, indicating four places that had been set while Emily was out of the room. "I'll get your food. Danny, want to give me a hand?"

As everyone took their seats, Emily noticed that Caro had managed to switch chairs with Penny. Now she was sitting next to Eric. She gave him her most dazzling smile.

"So you're going to Saratoga. What fun! I went there with my parents a few years ago. Of course, I was a mere *child* then. I just *adored* watching all the beautiful horses. They're in Europe right now."

Eric blinked. "The horses?"

Caro's trill of laughter was like the tinkling of little bells. "No, silly! My parents! Oh, here's your lunch," she said as Danny put a plate in front of him. "You just go right ahead and eat. I'm sure you must be terribly hungry. I mean, you look like

23

an athlete, and athletes have to keep up their strength."

As Caro chattered merrily on, Judy leaned over and whispered to Emily, "Is she for real?"

"Amazing, isn't it?" Emily whispered back. "And just look at Eric! He's falling for her hook, line, and sinker."

It seemed she was right. As Eric devoured his meal, his eyes never left Caro's face. It was as if he'd never seen a girl before. Emily had a hard time keeping a straight face as she finished her own lunch and joined in the general conversation around the table. Judy fit right in, she was happy to see—not that Emily had ever doubted she would. Still, she was glad when the meal was over, and the Thoros started clearing away the dishes. She couldn't wait to show off the rest of the camp. And most of all, she couldn't wait to introduce Judy and her family to Joker!

Libby leaped up and handed Judy's crutches to her. Lynda and Danny accompanied Emily's mother and father out of the dining room, closely followed by Penny and Dru, while Pam went to help Marie in the kitchen. On her way out, Emily paused by her brother's chair. Eric didn't seem to notice that everybody else had left. He was still staring at Caro, and Caro was still talking a mile a minute, telling him all about Field Day, and Libby's grandmother's visit. Emily waited patiently for her to take a breath, and when she did, she tapped Eric on the shoulder.

"Eric, want to see the rest of the camp?" Emily asked.

"Huh? The camp?" Eric looked at his sister as though he was trying to remember who she was. "Uh . . . sure. Yeah, I'd like to see it . . . " he mumbled.

Caro stood up, brushing invisible crumbs from her pink flowered shorts and smoothing back a loose strand of pale blond hair. "Oh, Eric, I'm so sorry! I didn't mean to keep you away from Emily and your parents. But I've just been so *fascinated* by our conversation. . . . "

No wonder, Emily thought. The only person who had been talking was Caro herself, and nobody's conversation was more interesting to Caro than Caro's.

"Why don't I tag along?" Caro said with another of those radiant smiles that immediately reduced Eric to jelly. "I promise I won't be in the way. You don't mind, do you, Emily?"

"No, I don't mind," Emily said, grinning at Eric. "And I bet Eric doesn't mind, either. But if you're coming, let's go. I want to show them everything!"

Chapter Three

Emily's parents, Judy, and the rest of the Fillies were waiting outside when Emily, Eric, and Caro came out of the dining room. Judy and Libby had their heads together, giggling and talking a mile a minute. That made Emily very happy—Judy was her best friend from home, and Libby was her best friend at camp, and she was glad the two girls liked each other. When she'd first met Libby, the bouncy little redhead had reminded her of Judy. They were both bubbly, full of fun and mischief. Judy would have had such a great time at Webster's, if only she hadn't broken her leg! But even though she was only here for a few days, and she wouldn't be able to ride, Emily was determined to make sure that Judy had the time of her life.

"Well, there you are!" Mr. Jordan said as Emily

joined them all. "We were beginning to think you'd deserted us."

Emily laughed. "No way! I just had to wake up Eric."

"Wake him?" Mrs. Jordan echoed. Then she saw Eric and Caro, and smiled. "Oh, I see what you mean. Eric seems to be quite taken with Princess Caroline."

"Mom!" Emily hissed. "She's not supposed to know we call her that!"

"Sorry, honey," her mother whispered. "It just slipped out because that's what you always call her in your letters."

"First things first," Judy said, hopping over to Emily on her crutches. "The horses! I'm *dying* to see the horses, and most of all, I'm dying to see Joker, the most beautiful horse in the world!"

"Foxy's beautiful, too," Libby put in, giving Emily a mock scowl. "But to hear Emily talk, you'd think the sun rises and sets on Joker."

Emily widened her eyes and said innocently, "Doesn't it?"

"Oh, get away!" Libby poked her in the ribs. "C'mon, let's take Judy and your folks to the stables. We can move Judy into the bunkhouse later."

"I'm going back to the cabin—gotta write a letter home," Lynda said. "Nice meeting you, Mr. and Mrs. Jordan. Catch you later, okay? Danny, you coming?"

"Sure," Danny said. "See you later," she said to Emily's parents. Penny and Dru decided to visit the mares and foals, so Emily, Judy, Emily's parents, and Libby headed toward the stables, with Eric and Caro trailing behind.

"This is exactly the way you described it, Emily," Judy said as they walked down the path to the stables. "I feel like I've been here all along!"

Emily led the way into the stable where the horses and ponies were placidly munching their hay and feed. As they passed each stall, Emily and Libby announced the name of the animal inside and who it had been assigned to for the summer. Libby stopped in front of Foxy's stall.

"This is *my* horse," she said proudly, putting her arms around Foxy's neck when he stuck his head out over the door. "Foxy's a terrific jumper. I've been riding him for years. I don't know how much you know about horses," she added, turning to Mr. and Mrs. Jordan, "but Foxy's really great. He's a light bay, almost a sorrel, but he has classic bay markings—black mane and tail, and the cutest black tips to his ears!"

Foxy nibbled at her midriff, and Libby giggled. "Stop that, silly! Here, have a sandwich." She pulled a flattened, barely recognizable object from her hip pocket and offered it to Foxy on the palm of her hand. He gobbled it up immediately.

"I didn't know horses ate sandwiches," Eric said. "Especially sandwiches like *that*. That's tuna, isn't it?"

"Foxy *loves* tuna," Libby assured him. "Foxy

loves everything. I gave him peanut butter and jelly once, and he ate it right up."

"Weird," said Eric.

Emily gave him a poke. "What's weird about it? *You* love tuna, and peanut butter and jelly, don't you?"

"Yeah, but I'm a person, not a horse," Eric pointed out.

Caro thought that was the cleverest thing anyone had ever said. She dissolved in giggles. "Oh, Eric, you say the *funniest* things!"

Eric blushed.

Emily strode ahead, stopping in front of Joker's stall. He stuck his head out, ears pricked forward, whuffling a gentle greeting. Emily patted his velvety nose, then pressed her cheek to his. Her eyes shining with love, she said, "*This* is Joker. *My* horse—for the summer, anyway."

"Gee, he really is something," Judy said, stroking Joker's glossy golden neck. "He's even more gorgeous than he looked in the photos you sent!"

"Nice to meet you, Joker," Mr. Jordan said. "Want to shake hooves or something?"

"Oh, Daddy!" Emily giggled.

Her mother patted the big palomino, saying, "Aren't you lucky that Matt assigned him to you!"

"I'm lucky, all right," Emily agreed. With a glance at Caro, she added, "And it was worth a fight to keep him."

But Caro didn't seem to hear, or else she'd forgotten all about trying to trick Emily into swapping horses with her during their very first week

at Webster's. Instead, she took Eric's hand and pulled him away from Joker's admirers to the next stall.

"This is Dark Victory, *my* horse," she told him as Vic poked his head out over the door. "Matt gave him to me because he's the best jumper at camp, and I'm the best rider. I won first place in the advanced jumping competition on Field Day last week."

"So did Vic," Libby reminded her. "You didn't go over all those jumps yourself, remember!"

Emily expected Caro to make some cutting remark in return, but the blond girl just smiled sweetly at Libby, and even more sweetly at Eric. "Libby's right," she said. "We're a team, Vic and I. Do you ride, Eric?"

Eric shook his head. "No, I'm not into horses. One horse nut in the family's enough, and that's Emily. She's been horse crazy ever since she was a little kid—she and Judy." He looked over at Emily and grinned. "I wouldn't be surprised if she decided to take Joker home with her at the end of the summer and turn our garage into a stable."

Emily turned to her father. "Hey, Daddy, you could always park in the street," she teased.

"Or I could just get rid of the car and ride Joker to work every morning," Mr. Jordan teased back. "But I don't think he'd be too happy in a parking lot all day—unless I parked him next to a Mustang or a Colt."

Everybody laughed. Then Emily said, "There's still so much more for you all to see. C'mon, I'll show you the riding rings, and then I'll take you down to the dock where we swim. And then we'll go back to the farmhouse and pick up Judy's bags and get her settled in the Fillies' cabin. And *then* there's water sports, and after that, we're going to have riding class—it's usually in the morning, but because of the trail ride it'll be this afternoon. You can all watch that. And *then*—"

"Whoa!" Judy cried. "I'll never be able to keep up on these crutches. Maybe we'd better pick up my wheelchair . . . only I hate to make somebody push me all over the place."

"How about the buggy?"

Chris Webster had been in the tack room, and he came out in time to hear what Judy said. Wiping his hands on his jeans, he said, "Hi. I'm Chris Webster. You're Judy, Emily's friend, right?"

Judy nodded and whispered to Emily, just as Emily knew she would, "He's really cute!"

"Hello, Chris," Mrs. Jordan said, shaking his hand. "I'm Emily's mother, and this is Mr. Jordan."

Chris grinned. "I remember you from the first day of camp." He shook hands with Mr. Jordan, then went on, "I could hitch up the buggy to old Sally—she's a good driving horse—and then Judy wouldn't have to worry about that wheelchair. I could drive her around."

"Oh, neat!" Judy said. "That would be the next best thing to actually riding a horse! I mean, if you don't mind."

"Hey, Chris, can I come, too? I can drive. Remember last year, when you let me drive Sally all over the farm?" Libby said eagerly.

"Yeah, I remember, all right! You got the buggy wheels stuck in the mud, and Warren and I had to pull you out!"

Libby made a face. "That's just because we'd had a whole week of rain. I was doing fine until then. Come on, Chris! I'll help you hitch Sally up, and then I'll just ride along and keep Judy company, okay?"

Chris shrugged. "Okay. But remember, *I'm* in the driver's seat. C'mon, Judy. Sally's stall is down at the end."

"We'll meet you at the riding rings," Emily called after them as Chris, Judy, and Libby headed for the far end of the stable. Turning to her parents, Eric, and Caro, she said, "Let's go, gang!"

After Emily had finished leading the way around the camp, Mr. Jordan and Eric went back to the farmhouse to pick up Judy's wheelchair and duffel bag. Mrs. Jordan went to chat with Marie, and Emily and Caro hurried off to the Fillies' cabin. Emily wanted to have Judy's bunk all ready for her when Chris brought her and Libby back— he was taking a detour by way of the west pasture so Judy could see the mares and foals.

"Why didn't you tell me you had such a cute brother?" Caro purred.

"I didn't think I had to," Emily replied. "I have

33

his picture along with Mom and Dad's tacked up over my bunk. You could have seen for yourself."

"I never really noticed . . . . Does Eric have a girlfriend back home?"

Emily was tempted to tell Caro that Eric had *seven* girlfriends, one for each day of the week, but instead she told the truth. "No, not really. He's not into dating much."

"I can't imagine why," Caro mused. "I'd think girls would be just *crazy* about him!"

Emily sighed. "Caro, my brother's going to be leaving tomorrow, and then he'll only be back long enough for my parents to pick up Judy. That's hardly enough time to get a romance going!"

Caro widened her big, beautiful eyes. "Who said anything about romance? I was just curious, that's all. Speaking of romance," she added, "I think Chris really likes your friend Judy."

Emily stared at her. "He just *met* her, for Pete's sake!"

"Haven't you ever heard of love at first sight?" Caro asked.

"You're bananas!" Emily said, shaking her head in astonishment.

"Oops, sorry! I forgot that Chris is *your* special friend," Caro replied with a little smirk.

Emily flushed. "You really *are* bananas! He's my friend, but he's not special—not in the way you mean."

"Then why are you blushing?"

"I am *not* blushing!" Emily said, turning even

redder. "Honestly, Caro, don't you know it's possible for a girl to be friends with a boy without him being her boyfriend?"

"I wonder if Chris knows you like him," Caro went on as though Emily hadn't spoken.

"*Caro!*" Emily stopped walking, put her hands on her hips, and faced Caro, glaring at her. "If you say *one word* to Chris, I'll . . . I'll—"

"You'll what?"

Emily's eyes narrowed. "Remember when you found the frog in your bunk the first night? And the bug a few nights later? Well, I saw a porcupine down by the sheep meadow the other day, and unless you want to turn into a *pincushion* the next time you go to bed, you'd just better keep quiet!"

"You wouldn't!" Caro gasped.

Emily smiled. "Try me," she said sweetly. "Now come on, if you're coming. I have to figure out where Judy's going to sleep."

She stomped into the bunkhouse, Caro at her heels. Lynda and Danny were playing cards on Lynda's bunk.

"Hi. Where's Judy?" Danny asked.

"Chris is giving her a buggy ride," Caro said, "and Libby went along as a chaperone!"

Lynda blinked. "Huh?"

"Never mind," Emily said quickly. "Dad and Eric will be here any minute with Judy's stuff, so we have to decide where to put her."

"Well, during lunch Caro said Judy could have her bunk," Lynda reminded them.

Caro shook her head. "On second thought, I

couldn't *possibly* sleep in an upper bunk—heights make me dizzy. There's a scientific name for it, but I forget what it is."

"Hydrophobia?" Danny suggested with a perfectly straight face.

Emily and Lynda snorted with laughter as Caro scowled. "Very funny," she fumed. "I happen to know that hydrophobia is another word for rabies! And I don't really care what it's called, but I'm not switching bunks with Emily's friend." She stomped over to her bed and sat down. Whipping a nail file out of her pocket, she began shaping one already perfect fingernail.

"Hi, everybody!" Judy called out as she hobbled through the door on her crutches, followed by Libby. "I've never ridden in a buggy before— boy, is it fun! Chris even let me handle the reins for a few minutes."

"She did pretty well, too," Libby added. "At least she didn't get us stuck in the mud!"

"That's because there *wasn't* any mud," Judy said, laughing. "But if there was, I bet I'd have gotten stuck in it." She grinned at Emily. "Okay, where do I sleep? I'll sleep anywhere; I'm just so happy to be here!"

"I've got it all worked out," Emily said promptly. "You're going to take my bunk—it's a lower one, and you'll be bunkmates with Libby. I'll take the one over Caro's." She looked over at Caro to see her reaction, but Caro kept her attention on her fingernails.

Judy looked surprised. "I thought you didn't

like to sleep in an upper bunk because you were afraid you'd fall out."

"Not anymore," Emily said. "When I first came to Webster's I was afraid of a lot of things, but not now."

Emily showed Judy her bunk, and Judy sat down with a sigh. "Boy, am I out of shape! I've been sitting around doing nothing for so long that I'm really pooped right now." She looked up at the little ledge over Emily's bunk and frowned. "Hey, Emily, some friend you are!" she teased.

"What do you mean?" Emily asked.

"Well, you have pictures of your mom and dad, and Eric, and even Joker, but there's not a single one of me." She reached out and touched one of the model horses Emily had brought with her to camp. "I remember when you packed these," she said softly. "We had such great plans . . . . "

Emily sat down on the bed beside her. "For your information, I didn't put up a picture of you because I don't *have* a picture of you," she said. "Any time I ever took one, you'd say it made you look fat, or you didn't have any chin, or something, remember? And then you'd tear it up."

Libby, who had scrambled into the bunk above, hung her head over the edge. "You'll have to let Emily take one this week, Judy, so we can stick it up with all the others. See all those pictures on the walls?"

Judy looked around and nodded.

"Emily took them all. She's the official Fillies photographer, and you're kind of an official

Filly—or you would have been if you hadn't had that accident—so you belong up there, too."

Judy grinned. "Okay. But only from the knees up, and *without* those darned crutches!"

Emily knelt down and opened her camp trunk at the foot of the bunk, taking out her Polaroid camera. "Okay, Judy, this is it." She peered through the viewfinder. "Say 'cheese'!"

"Oh, no!" Judy squealed, grabbing the pillow and holding it over her face. "Not now—I'm not ready!"

"Judy the pillow-head!" Danny shouted, laughing, as Emily took the picture. The Fillies crowded around her, giggling as the camera spat out the picture.

"Hey, Judy, it's only from the knees up, just like you said," Lynda called out.

"It looks exactly like you!" Emily said solemnly, tossing the photo to Judy.

"You're right," Judy said, just as solemnly. "That is the *real* me. You have my permission to add it to your collection."

Emily shook her head. "Oh, no. I want one with your bare face hanging out. C'mon, Judy, smile!"

"I give up!" Judy grinned, and Emily snapped the shutter.

As the photograph developed, Emily groaned. "You crossed your eyes! Not fair!"

Lynda peered over her shoulder. "No, she didn't—she only crossed *one* eye. How'd you do that, Judy?"

Judy smirked. "I've been practicing. And believe me, it isn't easy!"

Just then there was a knock at the screen door.

"Baggage service," Emily's father called.

"Come on in," Emily answered. Mr. Jordan entered, carrying Judy's bag, and Eric followed, pushing the wheelchair.

"You can put Judy's duffel right over here on my camp trunk, Daddy," Emily said.

"Where do you want this thing?" Eric asked.

Judy wrinkled her nose. "I don't *want* it at all, but I guess I'll need it. How about over there in the corner by the bureau? And thanks, Mr. Jordan, Eric. I'm really sorry to be so much trouble."

"You're no trouble at all," Emily's father assured her. He looked around the cabin. "So this is where you live," he said to Emily. "It's exactly the way you described it. Your mother wants to see it, too, but she's still gabbing with Marie, so I guess she'll pay you a visit later."

While Emily showed Mr. Jordan and Judy the ribbons she'd won on Field Day, Caro got up off her bunk and came over to Eric.

"Water sports are next," she told him, fluttering her lashes. "I bet you're awfully hot, since you've been walking all around the camp. I'm sure it would be all right if you went swimming, too."

"Uh . . . well, I guess I am kind of warm. And I did bring my trunks . . . ."

"Wonderful!" Caro cooed. "You can change up at the farmhouse, and then I'll—*we'll* meet you down by the river."

"Yipes!" Lynda cried, looking at her watch. "We'd better hurry up, guys, or we'll be late."

"Then I think we'd better leave you young ladies," Mr. Jordan said. He gave Emily a kiss on the cheek. "See you down by the dock, honey."

As he and Eric left, Penny and Dru came dashing in and paused by Emily's bunk.

"Aren't the foals adorable?" Dru asked Judy happily.

"We saw you and Libby and Chris in the buggy," Penny added.

"They're pretty cute, all right," Judy replied as the rest of the girls began getting out of their riding clothes and putting on their bathing suits.

"Aren't you going to put on a suit, Judy?" Emily asked. "You could sit on the end of the dock and stick one foot into the water."

Judy shook her head. She looked a little pale, Emily thought, concerned. Or maybe it was just because everybody else was so tanned. "I think maybe I'd better stay here and rest a little," Judy said. "I'm really pretty tired."

Emily finished pulling on her tank suit and hovered over Judy's bunk. "You sure you'll be okay? I mean, I could stay with you if you want," she said.

"Nope, I'll be just fine. I'll probably go right to sleep, so I'd be pretty boring company," Judy told her. "And I want to be wide awake so I can watch your riding class."

"You have to watch mine, too," Libby said, leaping down from her upper bunk. "Lynda,

40

Caro, and I are in the advanced class, and Emily, Danny, and Penny are intermediates."

"I'm still just a beginner," Dru added shyly, "but you can watch my class, too, if you want."

"Dru won the award for Most Improved Rider the second week we were here," Penny put in. "And she hasn't fallen off once since our first trail ride!"

"I want to watch *all* the classes," Judy said drowsily. "But right now, I just want to sleep."

Emily lingered behind after the rest of the Fillies had grabbed their towels and started off for the river. She sat on the edge of Judy's bunk. "I'm so glad you're here!" she said. "It's almost as if you'd been here all the time, just the way we planned. And next year, we'll both be here for the whole summer—if you don't break your *other* leg, that is!"

Judy smiled. "I'm glad to be here, too. I've missed you a whole lot, Emily. This is the first summer in ten whole years we haven't been together every minute."

"Don't I know it!" Emily agreed. "Well, I have to go now. Have a good nap. See you in about an hour, okay?"

"Mmm hmmm . . . . " Judy rolled over and snuggled her head into the pillow. She was asleep before Emily was out the door.

Poor Judy, Emily thought as she hurried to catch up with her friends. It hadn't really struck her how tough this summer had been for Judy until she actually saw her on crutches, trying to

41

keep up with everybody else who had two good legs. No wonder she was all tired out!

Emily suddenly realized that in all the years she'd known Judy, this was the very first time her friend had been a follower rather than a leader. Judy had always paved the way—making new friends, trying new things—while Emily, less sure of herself and a little shy, had lagged behind. And now, everything was turned around. Funny, Emily thought, how things work out . . . .

Chapter Four

Emily was eager to show her parents and Eric how much her swimming and diving had improved since she'd come to Webster's. Melinda, the Foals' counselor, was also the water sports instructor, and she had helped Emily a lot over the past three weeks. Today Melinda was working with the youngest Foals who were still at the doggy-paddle stage, so the Fillies and the Thoros were basically on their own. Lynda challenged Libby, Emily, Danny, and a few of the Thoros to a race from the dock to the float and back, and Emily swam with all her might, using the Australian crawl that she had finally mastered. She didn't win, but she came in a respectable fourth behind Lynda, Nancy, and Libby.

"Honey, you were terrific!" Mrs. Jordan said as Emily climbed back on the dock at the end of the race. She and Emily's father had been watching from the bank, and so had Eric, although Eric's attention had been distracted most of the time by Caro in her tropical-print bikini.

But even Eric said, "Hey, sis, you weren't half-bad."

Emily aimed a poke at his shoulder and missed as he dodged away. "Yeah, I know—I wasn't *half* bad, so what you mean is, I was *all* bad, right?" But she knew that wasn't what he meant at all. He was proud of her, she could tell. "You know," Eric went on, "I bet now you're as good a swimmer as Judy."

Emily beamed. "When she gets that cast off her leg, we'll have a race and then we'll find out!"

"Where *is* Judy?" Mr. Jordan asked.

"She's taking a nap. She was pretty tired after the drive up here, and from looking around camp," Emily said. "She wanted to rest up so she could be wide awake to watch our riding class."

Mrs. Jordan sighed. "I hope this trip won't be too much for Judy. But she wanted to come so badly, and her parents agreed that it would be a good idea. Emily, you must keep an eye on Judy while she's at Webster's." She smiled at her daughter, who was hopping on one foot to get the water out of her ears. "Kind of a change, isn't it? You looking out for Judy, I mean."

Emily nodded. "I was just thinking about that. Judy always used to look out for *me*." She grinned. "So I guess I owe her one."

"Come on, Eric," Caro said, twisting her silky

blond hair into a knot and fastening it with a barrette on the top of her head. "Let's swim out to the float, now that all the jocks have finished their race." She pouted prettily. "I hope you don't mind that I'm not a jock—I just *hate* competition among girls in sports."

"Oh, no. I don't mind at all," Eric said. "I mean, all those girls who lift weights and stuff to develop their muscles—well, I mean, girls ought to be *girls*, you know?"

Emily groaned inwardly. She really hated seeing her big, handsome brother making a fool of himself over Caro, but there was nothing she could do about it. She just hoped that Eric wouldn't be completely taken in by Caro's sweet, helpless act. Caro was about as helpless as a barracuda, and talk about competitive! When it came to riding, Caro was as competitive as they came. But Eric didn't know that—yet.

Emily didn't have much time to worry about Eric and Caro. Rachel, the Thoros' counselor who was also the camp's athletic coach, arrived and started rounding up players for a volleyball game. She persuaded Emily's mother and father to play, one on each side, and the minute Caro and Eric came out of the water, she talked Eric into playing, too. When she approached Caro, Caro just smiled and said, "Rachel, you know how *hopeless* I am at sports. I'll lead the cheering section."

Emily found herself on her father's team, opposite her mother and Eric. Once the game started, she was amazed at her mother's athletic ability. Mrs. Jordan made point after point, leaping around like a teenager. Emily glanced around at her teammates, wondering if they thought it was weird that her mother could spike the ball as well as any of them. But they didn't seem to. Fillies and Thoros alike whooped and cheered, accepting both Mr. and Mrs. Jordan as members of the teams. As for Eric, most of the Thoros obviously thought he was absolutely fantastic. Emily decided that she probably had the neatest family of any girl at Webster's, and she glowed with pride for her parents and her brother. If only Judy could be there . . . .

But that was silly. Judy *was* there, right over in the Fillies' bunkhouse, sound asleep in Emily's bed. How could she forget?

"Emily! Wake up! You missed a perfectly easy shot—it came right at you," Rachel yelled.

"Sorry," Emily shouted. From then on, she concentrated on the game, and even scored a point, much to her brother's surprise. When it was over and Emily's team had won, he trotted over and punched her lightly on the arm.

"Looks like my little sister's turning into a jock," he teased. "When she can keep her mind on the game, that is."

Emily could hardly believe it. Two compliments in one day from Eric! She couldn't remember him ever telling her she'd done anything well before. Maybe that was because she'd never been good at anything he was interested in. And speaking of interest, Emily thought as Eric went straight past her to Caro's side, he sure is interested in Caro, and Caro seems to like him a lot, too. But Caro likes *all* boys, so that doesn't really mean anything . . . does it?

Well, it's none of my business anyhow, Emily decided, and joined her parents, who were catching their breath and talking to Rachel. Rachel looked up as Emily came over, and said, "I was just telling your parents that they should have been here last weekend for Field Day when I was sick. We wouldn't have had to cancel the volleyball game with the Long Branch boys, and we'd probably have won if your mom and dad were on our team."

Mrs. Jordan laughed. "Thanks, Rachel, but I don't imagine the rules allow a pair of old folks like us to compete in something like that."

"Mom, want to come to the cabin with me?" Emily asked. "You haven't seen it yet."

"Why don't you do that, Meg?" her father said. "I think I'll take a stroll along the riverbank and meet you at the riding ring for Emily's class."

"Yeah, Mrs. Jordan, come see where we live," Libby said as she and Lynda passed by on their way to the cabin.

"I'd love to," replied Mrs. Jordan. "And maybe I could wash up and fix my hair. I must look a mess."

"You look great, Mom," Emily assured her. "But feel free to use our bathroom. We'd better hurry, though. The rest of us have to change into our riding clothes and saddle up our horses, and Pam hates it if we're late for class.''

A short while later, Emily and the other Fillies, dressed in jeans, boots, and hard hats, were on their way to the stables—that is, all the other Fillies except one. Caro was still blow-drying her hair while Judy and Emily's mother kept her company. She dashed into the stable to saddle Vic as the rest of the campers were heading for the training rings, and caught up with the advanced group just in time. Emily saw her parents, Eric, and Judy sitting on the bleachers between the advanced ring and the intermediate one. Judy and Mr. and Mrs. Jordan smiled and waved at her, but Eric had turned around and was staring at Caro.

"All right, girls," Pam called from the center of the ring. "Heads up, backs straight. Walk your horses, and when I give the signal, slow-trot.''

The riders circled the ring at a walk, then urged their mounts into a trot at Pam's command. When Pam told them to canter, Emily had no problem getting Joker on the right lead. As usual, he did everything perfectly, but Emily thought he was even more perfect than usual this afternoon, as though he knew he had a very special audience and was showing off just a little.

"Feel the outside rein, Meghan," Pam called. "Penny, shoulders back—don't lean over . . . . Very good, Emily. Okay, now reverse and trot!''

After the riders had put their horses through their paces for about fifteen minutes, Chris came

into the ring and helped Pam set up the jumps. They positioned the rails two feet off the ground, higher than they had ever been before, Emily noticed. She glanced over at Judy, who was leaning forward eagerly, eyes shining. One of the things they had both wanted most to learn at Webster's was jumping. When they'd talked about it back home, Emily had been sure that Judy would be really good at it, while she herself would probably foul up, or fall off. And now here she was on Joker's back, filled with confidence and pride, and like Joker, ready to show off for the benefit of Judy and her parents.

In fact, Emily was so anxious to impress them that when it was her turn to take Joker around the course, she let him approach the first jump much too fast. He cleared it easily, but was off stride when he reached the second one and knocked down the rail with his hind hooves. Emily managed to slow him down in time to sail over the third and last jump with inches to spare, but she knew she hadn't done well. So did Pam.

"Where's the fire, Emily?" Pam yelled. "This isn't a steeplechase, you know. You lost control there for a minute, didn't you?"

Blushing, Emily nodded.

"Next time take it slow and easy," Pam told her as Emily slackened Joker's pace to a trot, then a walk. "Remember, *you're* supposed to be in charge here, not Joker. He loves to jump so much that he thinks he can fly, but you have to set the pace. Okay, Danny, you're next."

That's what you get for showing off, Emily told herself. She leaned over and patted Joker's shoulder, saying to him, "Sorry, fella. I'll do better next time, honest."

And she did. On her second round, Emily concentrated on everything she'd been taught—seat out, weight in thighs, knees, and stirrups, hands even and light on the reins. This time Pam called out, "That's the way! I knew you could do it," and Emily heaved a sigh of relief. Joker did, too, she was sure.

The next time she looked over at the bleachers, her parents and Eric were gone, but Judy was still there. When Judy caught her eye, she grinned and threw her arms in the air, clasping her hands together over her head in a gesture of triumph. As Emily circled the ring, she could see Eric leaning over the fence watching the advanced class, and her mother and father over at the beginners' ring watching Dru in action. They all came back, though, to catch the end of Emily's class.

Mr. and Mrs. Jordan were beaming when they met her at the gate to the intermediate ring.

"My goodness, Emily," her mother said, "you're really a *very* good rider!"

"You sure are, honey," her father added. "I took some pictures of you going over those jumps. Hope they come out all right. Your horse was going so fast that they'll probably be kind of blurry, though."

For the first time, Emily noticed her father's camera on a strap around his neck. "That's okay.

The reason he was going so fast was because I lost control, like Pam said. Did you get any shots of the second round?" she asked hopefully. "That time we did it just right!"

"I used up the whole roll on your class, and on the others, too," Mr. Jordan told her.

"Did you get any shots of Caro—I mean, the advanced riders?" Eric asked.

"Yep. I got Caro, and Libby, and Lynda, and a couple of that little Filly in the Beginners' class—what's her name?"

"Dru," Emily said. "Can you have them developed real fast and send them to me?"

Mrs. Jordan laughed. "Hey, why do *you* need photographs? You have the real thing. Daddy and I need those pictures to remind us what you look like!" She reached up and touched Emily's knee. "We miss you a lot, you know. You've never been away from home for a whole summer before."

"I know." Emily covered her mother's hand with her own. "I miss you, too. But I'd really like some prints to add to our collection."

Judy, who had been leaning on her crutches while Emily's family surrounded her and Joker, came forward. She put an arm around Joker's neck and rested her cheek against him the way Emily often did. "You looked great out there," she told Emily. "When you were taking Joker over those jumps, I was pretending it was me. But next year . . ."

Emily smiled at her. "Next year we'll do it together."

"Emily, move it!" Danny called, trotting past her on Misty. "Fillies are supposed to set up for supper tonight, so we have to make tracks for the farmhouse!"

"Gotta go," Emily said, gathering Joker's reins. She paused before riding off. "You're going to be here for supper, right?" she asked her parents.

"Afraid not, honey," Mrs. Jordan said. "We have a reservation at the Riverside Hotel in Winnepac, and we really have to check in. So I guess we won't see you again until we come back from Saratoga."

Caro trotted up on Vic in time to hear Emily's mother's words.

"All three of you?" she asked. When Mr. Jordan nodded, she looked down at Eric. "Wouldn't you like to stay for supper and the campfire? It's really fun—the campfire, I mean. Although supper's not too terrible, either," she added with a smile.

Eric looked from his father to his mother, then said, "Well, if somebody could get me back to the hotel . . ."

"No problem," Caro said promptly. "I'm sure Matt or Warren could drive you into town."

"Fine by me," Mr. Jordan said. "But we should hit the road pretty soon." Emily leaned down so he could give her a farewell kiss. "See you on Sunday, Emily. I'll try to have the prints by then."

"Okay, Daddy. See you Sunday. You're really going to love the dressage exhibition," Emily said. "There's a couple who have a stable nearby, and they both studied at the Viennese Riding

53

School, where the Lippizaners are trained." Mr. Jordan looked blank. "You know, those beautiful white stallions that leap in the air and do all sorts of wonderful dances?"

"Right. Sure," her father said. "Sounds good. Meg, you ready?"

"Yes, dear." Mrs. Jordan kissed Emily, too, gave Judy a hug, and she and Mr. Jordan headed for their car.

"I'll meet you guys at the stable," Judy told Libby and Emily, and she began hobbling on her crutches in that direction.

As Emily nudged Joker with her heels and started for the stable, she heard Caro saying to Eric, "I'm *so* glad you're staying. We can really get to know each other better."

Emily glanced at Libby, who was riding next to her on Foxy. She could tell from Libby's expression that they were thinking the same thing: If Eric got to know Caro better, would he still like her as much?

Judy wanted to help the Fillies prepare supper, so Marie sat her down at the kitchen table and gave her a big basket filled with string beans that the Foals had picked earlier in the day.

"Just cut off the ends and put the beans in this colander," Marie told her. "Then we'll rinse them and steam them."

"I could help you," Dru offered.

Judy grinned. "Thanks. I've never seen so many beans in my life. If I did them all by myself, we'd probably be having beans for breakfast, because I'd never get them done in time for supper!"

"Beans for breakfast—yuck!" Dru said with a giggle.

"If we had them, you'd eat them," Caro said over her shoulder on her way to the dining room with a basketful of silverware. "You'll eat anything!"

"Caro . . ." Marie warned.

"I'm that way, too," Judy said cheerfully. "You know what I really *love* for breakfast?"

Dru shook her head. Before Judy could reply, Emily called out from where she stood at the kitchen sink, "Leftover salad!"

"You're kidding!" Dru was astonished. "That's even yuckier than string beans!"

Judy laughed. "Want to know what Emily's favorite food is?"

"What?"

"Twinkies!" Judy said at the exact same moment as Emily said, "Devil Dogs!"

"Since when?" Judy asked, surprised. "It always used to be Twinkies."

Emily shrugged. "Not anymore. I've decided I like Devil Dogs better. I've been on a chocolate kick lately. Maybe it's because of Marie's great brownies."

"Yeah, Marie makes the world's most fantastic brownies," Dru said with a sigh. "I think that's really *my* favorite food."

"Are we having them for dessert tonight?" Judy asked hopefully.

"Sorry, Judy, tonight it's peach pie," Marie told her. "Brownies tomorrow night, I promise."

"I love peach pie, too," Judy said. "I love *everything*! But more than anything else, I love being here at Webster's with all of you. Hey, look at this, Dru! We've finished more than half the beans. Only about a zillion more to go!"

Chapter Five

"You're really gonna love campfire, Judy," Libby said later that evening as she and Emily walked on either side of Judy, slowing their pace to hers. They were on their way to the picnic grove where most of the other campers had already gathered. Distant voices and laughter drifted through the peaceful summer air, and the sky above glowed orange, red, and gold as the sun set behind the mountains. Emily felt she couldn't possibly be happier. Everything was absolutely perfect. Here she was, with her two best friends, at her favorite time of day, at Webster's Country Horse Camp. What more could she want? She grinned at Judy, and Judy grinned back.

"You've described everything at Webster's in your letters—including campfire—so I know just what it's going to be like," Judy said. "And you wrote about how beautiful it is here at sunset, but it's even *more* beautiful than you said." She turned to Libby. "Is there a special program tonight, or will we all just sing?"

"Oh, we always sing," Libby told her, "but tonight I think we're going to play charades. You know what that is, don't you?"

"Sure I do! That's when you have two teams, and each team thinks up things for the other guys to act out without using words," Judy said.

"Judy's terrific at charades," Emily said. "She's much better than I am. Let's all try to get on the same team, okay?"

"Okay! What about Eric?" Libby asked. "Is he good at it, too?"

Emily shrugged. "Search me. I've never played with him. But he doesn't like games much. I doubt if he'll want to play."

Judy giggled. "If he does, what do you bet he'll be on Caro's team? She's really knocked him for a loop."

"Has she ever!" Emily sighed.

"Hey, Emily, I think you're being too rough on Caro," Judy said. "I know how she tried to take Joker away from you and everything, but she doesn't seem to be nearly as bad as you made her out to be in your letters."

"Believe me, I *know* Caro and you don't," Emily said. "But it doesn't really matter. Tomorrow he'll be taking off for Saratoga, and Caro will forget about him the minute he's gone."

The three girls had reached the campfire site,

and the Fillies waved wildly as soon as they saw them. Dru had saved a place for Judy next to her on a fallen log, and Emily and Libby sat down on the ground between Lynda and Penny. Eric was beside Caro, close to the fire. She was whispering in his ear, and Eric had a silly smile on his face.

Marie stood up from where she had been sitting with Melinda and the Foals, and moved into the light cast by the burning logs.

"Before we start playing charades," she said, "I think it would be nice if we welcomed Judy Bradford. Judy was supposed to spend the summer with us, but she had an accident, so she's only here for the rest of this week. Let's give her a big hand, okay?"

All the Foals, Thoros, and Fillies clapped, and Emily clapped harder than anybody. Judy blushed and waved one crutch in the air.

"Thanks, everybody," she said. "Next year, my friend Emily and I are going to come back, and when we do, I hope I see all of you again. I don't have everybody's names straight yet, but I'll figure out who's who real soon. And I hope you'll all remember *me* next summer, even without these darned crutches!"

All the campers applauded again and so did Emily. She'd never known anybody who could turn a group of strangers into friends as quickly as Judy could. That was why Judy was so popular back home. Because she liked people, people liked her. And because Emily was Judy's best friend, everyone liked Emily, too. Only now,

Emily thought, it was different. *Emily* was the one everybody had known first, and she had gotten to be their friend on her own.

"Time for charades," Marie said after the applause had died down. "For those of you who don't know how to play, here's how it goes. We're all going to divide up into four teams. The idea of the game is for the members of each team to come up with phrases, or titles of books, movies, TV shows, whatever, and then give one to each member of the opposing team. Each girl has to *act out* whatever she's been given, and the rest of her team has to figure out what it is."

"We can't talk at all?" a Foal asked.

"Nope. Not one word!"

"Wow! That's going to be hard," another Foal sighed. "How do we tell who wins?"

"The team that makes the most correct guesses is the winner," Marie explained. "But there aren't any big prizes or anything. This is just for fun. Okay, campers, form your teams!"

Emily, Judy, and Danny ended up on a team with Penny, Dru, a Thoro named Janet, and a freckle-faced Foal. Their opponents were Caro, Libby, Lynda, a Foal, and Ellen and Beth, two Thoros. Emily's group huddled together, trying to think of things that their opponents would find hard to act out.

"But nothing impossible, remember," Judy said. "It's like Marie said—this game is *fun,* not tough competition."

"*National Velvet,*" Danny said promptly, naming her favorite book, but Emily shook her head.

"Too hard, Danny. Even if the girl who gets it pantomimes opening a book and starts galloping around the campfire, they'll never guess it."

"But we *do* want to win," Janet said. "And if the other members of their team can't guess what it is, we will."

"Fun, Janet," Judy reminded her. "It's supposed to be *fun.*"

"What about 'Little Red Riding Hood'?" the Foal piped up.

"Now that's a good one, Jenny," Judy told her, smiling, and the little girl beamed with pleasure.

Emily thought, *I've been here three whole weeks, and I didn't know that kid's name.* But that was one of the wonderful things about Judy—she had a memory like an elephant. For the first time, Emily wondered if elephants really had fantastic memories. Who could tell?

Emily glanced over at the opposing team. Her brother was bending over Caro's shoulder, apparently making suggestions, though he wasn't playing. Emily had never seen him pay so much attention to a girl before.

"We're ready," Libby shouted a few minutes later. "Who's first on your team?"

"Me," Janet said, and Libby handed her a slip of paper. Janet looked at it and grinned. "No problem!" She pantomimed singing by opening her mouth and flinging out one arm, then made a big circle with both arms.

"Song title," Judy translated. "The whole thing."

Now Janet glanced up at the sky and held out a hand. She made a face, and acted out opening an umbrella, then holding it over her head. Next she began walking around, pantomiming singing again.

" 'Singing in the Rain'!" Danny cried out.

Janet jumped up and down. "You got it!" she said, laughing.

Then it was the other team's turn, and Caro stood up. Emily knew she'd been given *Little House on the Prairie,* and soon Caro's teammates knew it, too. She had a little trouble with *prairie,* but the rest of it was clear sailing.

The two teams were neck and neck when Emily's turn came up. The minute she looked at her slip of paper, she knew she was in trouble. How could she ever act out *Charlotte's Web?* She glanced up and saw Caro and Eric with their heads close together. They were both grinning, and Emily guessed that the title had been their idea. Talk about impossible!

"What is it, Emily? Book, movie, song?" Judy asked.

Well, might as well give it her best shot. Emily pantomimed opening a book. Now what?

"They'll never get it!" Emily heard Caro say to Eric with a giggle.

"Come on, Emily," Janet called. "Whole thing? First word? What?"

Emily pantomimed "the whole thing." She decided the only thing to do was act out Charlotte, the spider, and hope somebody would catch on. Emily dropped down on all fours and began scuttling around the circle, wishing she had four more legs.

"Cat?"

"Dog?"

"Horse?"

"Squirrel?"

Emily shook her head vigorously. Better try again. This time she bent her elbows and knees, hoping she looked spiderlike.

"Dog with four broken legs!" Jenny shouted.

"I never heard of that book," Danny laughed.

Emily stood up, brushing her short brown hair out of her eyes. This was getting nowhere fast, and she was feeling sillier by the minute. She'd better forget about the spider for the moment and work on *web*. Emily held up two fingers.

"Second word," Judy said.

Now Emily started moving her right hand back and forth in front of her in a waving motion, trying to get across the idea of weaving.

"Ocean?" Danny guessed.

"Waves?" Janet suggested.

Emily groaned and rolled her eyes.

"Seasick!" Judy yelled, and everybody on both teams broke up.

Emily shook her head again. Then she realized that spiders didn't really *weave* webs—they *spun* them. She held up two fingers again to indicate

63

that she was still working on the second word, then began to whirl around as fast as she could.

"Turn?"

"Whirl?"

"Merry-go-round?"

"Dizzy?"

Emily stopped spinning and tried to focus on her teammates. She was dizzy, all right, and the other girls looked more confused than ever.

"Give up?" Ellen asked hopefully.

"No!" Janet shouted. "Give it one more try, Emily."

In desperation, Emily mimed the symbol for *whole thing* again. There was only one other way she could think of to get the idea across. She began making the gestures that went with the song, "The Inky-Dinky Spider," and by the time she'd pantomimed "Up came the sun and dried up all the rain," they had it—kind of.

"Spider!" Judy cried. "The Inky-Dinky Spider!"

"That's not a book," Jenny said.

"I know—Spiderman!" Janet yelled.

"That's a *comic* book. You're not doing a comic book, are you, Emily?" Danny asked.

Emily threw up her arms in surrender. "No, I'm not," she sighed.

"*Now* do you give up?" Caro asked, and when Emily's team admitted they were stumped, she said triumphantly, "*Charlotte's Web*!"

There was a chorus of groans. As Emily sat down, Danny said, "That was a really hard one,

Emily. I don't think anybody could have acted it out!"

Then it was Libby's turn. She breezed through "The Headless Horseman" with no difficulty, which meant that her team was ahead.

"My turn next," Judy said. She beamed at her teammates and their opponents as she hobbled forward on her crutches. Obviously she knew exactly what she was going to do. She mimed the symbol for *book*, then made a cranking motion next to her ear for *movie*.

"It's a book *and* a movie," Danny said.

Judy made a big circle with her arms, indicating the whole title. She threw back her head and pretended to howl while she beat on her chest with both fists. It wasn't easy, since she was leaning on her crutches, but she managed it. Then she pantomimed grabbing onto something with one hand and scratching herself like an ape with the other, still howling. Suddenly Emily remembered Libby swinging on the rope over the pool at Willoughby Falls.

"Tarzan!" she shouted, and Judy whooped with delight.

"That's it!" Judy shouted. "You got it!" The rest of their team clapped, and Emily didn't feel quite as dumb as she had when nobody had been able to guess her title.

By the time the game was over, it was clear that Emily's team had lost. But that didn't faze Judy at all. Smiling at their opponents, she said, "You may be better at charades, but I bet *we're* better

at toasting marshmallows!" Cheering, the girls all raced to join the other campers by the fire. They picked up toasting forks or long, sharpened sticks, stabbing the marshmallows Melinda had put out and holding them over the dancing flames.

Emily went over to where Eric was sitting next to Caro and poked him gently with the toe of her sneaker. "*Charlotte's Web,* huh?" she said with a mock glare. "Couldn't you have picked something a little harder?"

"Who, me?" Eric said innocently. "What do I know about spiders? That was Caro's idea."

"Oh, Eric, you're *terrible*!" Caro giggled. "It was not, and you know it!" She presented him with a perfectly toasted marshmallow. "Here, eat this and stop teasing your little sister."

Since Eric seemed to have forgotten she was there, Emily looked around for somewhere to sit, hoping there would be a space next to Judy. But Judy was between Libby and Penny, talking and laughing a mile a minute, so she sat down next to Lynda and concentrated on toasting her marshmallow.

"What's the matter, Emily?" Lynda asked. "You're awfully quiet."

Emily looked up. "Nothing's the matter. Guess I'm a little tired, that's all."

"Yeah, it's been a long day," Lynda said. "You must be real glad that Judy's here, though. I know how much you've missed her. She's really terrific! It's like she's been here all along—she's so friendly and everything. You're lucky to have a friend like Judy."

"I know it," Emily said. Then she looked at her marshmallow. "Rats! It's all burnt!"

"I love the burnt part," Lynda said cheerfully. "Let me peel off the outside, then you can toast it again."

Emily sighed. "Be my guest."

Chris Webster suddenly appeared near the campfire, his guitar slung over his shoulder on its strap, and struck a chord. Everybody looked up expectantly.

"Anybody want to sing?" he asked.

Everybody did, and several of the campers shouted out requests for their favorite songs. Chris began to play "Down in the Valley," and all the girls began to sing:

"Down in the valley, valley so low,
Hang your head over, hear the wind blow.
Hear the wind blow, love, hear the wind
   blow,
Hang your head over, hear the wind
   blow. . . . "

Emily could hear Judy's high, clear voice ringing out over all the rest. Judy was a soprano in the Girls' Choral Group at school, and she had a really good voice.

"Hey, Judy, want to sing the next verse all by yourself?" Chris suggested, so Judy did:

"Roses love sunshine, violets love dew,
Angels in heaven know I love you.
All that I've done, love, I've done for your
   sake,
Put your arms round me, feel my heart
   break."

Everybody else joined in the chorus. Even with their mouths full of marshmallows, their voices sounded great. The crickets were chirping, the cicadas were buzzing, and the moon was sailing high overhead. Everything was absolutely perfect. So why was Emily feeling so peculiar?

"Chris, would you let me try to play your guitar?" Judy asked. "Just for a little bit—I only started lessons a few weeks ago."

Emily stared at her in surprise. Judy hadn't told her that she was taking guitar lessons.

Chris shrugged and handed Judy his guitar. She put the strap over her shoulder and strummed a few chords.

"I'm just a beginner," she said, smiling at everybody, "but I'm really into it. I mean, when you're sitting around with your leg in a cast, you have to do *something,* right?" She looked over at Emily. "One of the songs I've been practicing a lot is 'White Coral Bells.' Emily and I like it a lot. Let's give it a try, okay?"

She strummed a few chords, then began to play and sing, and all the campers joined in:

"White coral bells upon a slender stalk,
Lilies of the valley deck our garden walk.
Oh, how I wish that I could hear them ring
That will happen only when the fairies sing."

They'd sung it so often that nobody had to be told to do it in rounds. When the last voices died away in the evening air, Judy handed the guitar back to Chris.

"For a beginner, you play pretty well," Chris said. He smiled at Judy, and Emily felt a funny kind of tight sensation in her stomach. Chris wasn't her boyfriend—far from it. But as Caro had said, he was a *special* kind of friend. And now he seemed to be Judy's special friend, too. Everybody seemed to have suddenly become Judy's special friend in just one day. And that was wonderful, Emily told herself—wasn't it?

"How come you never told me about guitar lessons in your letters?" Emily asked Judy a little later that night. Campfire was over, Matt had driven Eric—and Caro, who had begged so prettily to come along that Matt couldn't refuse—to the Riverside Hotel, and everyone else was on their way back to their cabins. Emily and Judy were walking side by side behind the rest of the Fillies.

Judy shrugged. "Oh, I don't know. Maybe because when you came home I wanted to surprise you with how well I could play." She grinned a little ruefully. "In spite of what Chris said, I know

70

I'm not very good yet, but by the end of the summer I'll be much better." She laughed. "At least I'll be able to play something besides 'White Coral Bells'! So far, it's the only song I know!"

Emily laughed, too. "I thought you sounded fine. And you sure surprised me, all right."

"It's like I told everybody before," Judy said. "If I didn't have anything to do except read your letters and wish I were here at Webster's with you, I'd go nuts. It's been pretty lonely without you, you know," she added softly.

"I've missed you, too," Emily said. The odd sensation in Emily's stomach completely disappeared. She and Judy were still best friends, and nothing would ever change that.

Chapter Six

The next morning, Emily woke up before any of the other Fillies, as she always did. She quietly put on her T-shirt, jeans, and boots. She loved to visit Joker all by herself in the pasture where the horses spent the night—it was so peaceful there, and Emily enjoyed being the only human being in a world of horses. As she tiptoed across the cabin floor, she paused for a moment by Judy's bunk, wondering if she should ask her friend to come with her. But Judy was sleeping so soundly that Emily decided not to disturb her.

Once outside, Emily took a deep breath of the fresh, cool air and looked up at the pale blue sky. It was going to be another beautiful day, and she was glad for Judy's sake, since she could only stay a short time. And tonight there was going to be a hayride. Judy would like that, Emily was sure.

Emily was looking forward to it herself—she'd missed the first one because she'd gone with Caro and the Thoros into Winnepac to hear Warren Webster's rock band at the American Legion Hall. As it turned out, Emily would have had a better time on the hayride. The rock concert wasn't all that much fun.

Walking across the dewy grass on her way to the pasture, Emily remembered the uncomfortable feelings she'd had the night before and laughed at herself. What had gotten into her, anyway? Well, whatever it was, it was gone now, and Emily couldn't wait to have a few minutes alone with her beloved horse.

But she wasn't alone. Somebody was standing by the pasture fence, leaning on the top rail and looking at the horses. Emily frowned. It was a boy, but he was too tall to be Chris, and too short to be Warren. Could it be one of the boys from Long Branch? That seemed unlikely at this early hour— or at any hour, for that matter.

As she came closer, she realized that there was something very familiar about him. The way he was standing, his thick brown hair . . .

"*Eric?*" she called out. "Eric, is that you?"

Her brother turned around and grinned sheepishly. "Uh . . . hi, Emily. Nice morning, isn't it?"

Emily trotted up beside him. "Eric, what in the world are you doing here? I thought Matt drove you to the hotel last night!"

"He did. And then he drove me back—Caro and me. I spent the night in Warren's room at the

73

farmhouse, since he went to Albany yesterday afternoon—something about some gigs his rock band is playing the next couple of nights . . . . " Eric was actually blushing. Emily couldn't ever remember seeing him blush before.

"Do Mom and Dad know you're here?" Emily asked, astonished. "Why *are* you here? What's going on?"

Eric bent down and carefully plucked a long blade of grass, which he stuck between his teeth. He chewed on it a little, then said, "Well, on the way into town, Mr. Webster—Matt—mentioned that since Warren wasn't going to be here for the next few days, he was going to have to hire somebody to help Chris finish up some repairs in the stables. And since I wasn't really crazy about hanging out with Mom and Dad at Saratoga, I said I was pretty handy with carpentry . . . . "

"And?" Emily said.

"And . . . well, he said if I was interested, he'd hire me, and he'd give me free room and board plus a few bucks, and Caro thought it was a good idea—"

"I bet she did!"

"Cut it out, Emily!" Eric spat out the blade of grass.

Emily widened her gray eyes innocently. "Cut *what* out?"

"You know what I mean. I just thought I'd give Chris a hand, that's all. So we talked to Mom and Dad, and they said okay, so here I am. And if you

74

say *one word* about Caro and me to *anybody,* I'll punch your lights out!"

Eric glowered at her, and Emily pretended to cower in fright. "Okay, okay!" she said. Then she giggled. "I never thought when I came to Webster's that *you'd* end up being a camper, too!"

"I'm *not* a camper!" Eric said. "I'm a carpenter, and don't you forget it."

Emily immediately put on a solemn expression. "I promise I won't forget it. And since you're here, you might as well say hello to Joker." She whistled long and low, the way Eric had taught her, and Joker raised his head and ambled toward her.

Emily slipped between the rails of the fence and put her arms around the palomino's neck. "Joker, you remember my brother, Eric, don't you? He doesn't know much about horses, but he's okay anyway." She led Joker over to where Eric was standing, and Eric reached out to pat his nose.

"Hi, Joker," he said. "Maybe while I'm here, somebody could give me a few pointers on how to ride—when I'm not helping Chris, that is."

"I'm sure *somebody* could," Emily said sweetly. "I'll bet Caro just might be able to find the time."

"Emily . . ." Eric warned.

Emily grinned. "Just a suggestion. Seriously, Eric, I think you'd probably be a good rider if you put your mind to it. You might even enjoy it."

"I'll think about it," Eric said. "Joker's a pretty neat horse, but I still like cars better." Joker tossed his head and stamped.

Emily made a face. "You've hurt his feelings. Besides, you're too young to have a driver's license, and you don't need a license to ride a horse." She looked at the other horses grazing in the field. "I know just the one for you. See that Appaloosa over there, next to the little sorrel?"

"Appa-*what*?" Eric said. "What's an Appa . . . whatever you just said?"

"Appaloosa," Emily repeated. "That's the black-and-white speckled horse standing beside the kind of reddish one."

"Well, why didn't you say so in the first place?"

"Sorry. I forgot what a dummy you are when it comes to horses," Emily teased. "Maybe I should have said, 'The black-and-white speckled model next to the reddish compact. Mint condition, about twelve years old. Four-legged drive, not much on speed, but good transportation.' "

Eric grinned. "Not bad, sis, not bad! Think I might be able to take it for a spin?"

"Hey, I'm just a salesman. You'll have to talk to the boss about that!"

Suddenly the clang of the big bell that hung outside the farmhouse rang out, calling the campers to breakfast. Emily looked at her watch.

"I didn't know it was so late. C'mon, Eric. Time for breakfast."

"If breakfast is anywhere near as good as lunch and supper, I can hardly wait," Eric said. "And even if it's not, I'm starved. Let's go!"

"Me, too!" Emily gave Joker a quick hug, then

77

climbed back over the fence. "Race you to the house!"

"Personally, I think your brother is one brick short of a load, like my grandmother says," Libby told Emily as they headed for the stables to saddle up their horses after breakfast. "Imagine giving up Saratoga and the races to stay here and work!"

"That's not the only reason he's staying, and you know it," Emily said. "It's Caro. He's fallen for her, hook, line, and sinker. I bet your grandmother says that, too!"

They both grinned, thinking of Libby's feisty little Gram.

"Hey, guys, wait up!" Judy was "crutching along" behind them, and both girls stopped so she could catch up.

"I thought you were busy talking to Chris," Libby said. "That's why we didn't wait."

"I was, but he and Eric took off to replace those rotting boards in the hayloft. And guess what!" Judy's eyes were shining with excitement.

"What?" Emily and Libby said together.

"During rest period after lunch, Chris is going to give me a driving lesson!"

"A driving lesson? You mean in a car?" Emily asked, amazed.

"No, silly! A *buggy* driving lesson. He's going to teach me how to drive Sally in the buggy. Isn't that neat?"

"That's neat, all right," Libby said, and Emily nodded.

"It's because I can't ride, and Chris knows how much I love horses, so he's going to teach me to drive." Judy beamed at Emily. "Even if I don't know how to jump and do all those things you've learned this summer, I'll at least learn how to do *something* with horses. And when you come home and we go back to The Barn, maybe I'll be able to teach you, too!"

"I don't think they have a buggy at The Barn," Emily said. The stable at home where she and Judy had been riding for the past year wasn't very well equipped. If they had a buggy, she'd never seen it. And even if they did, somehow she didn't like the idea of Judy showing her how to do something she hadn't learned at Webster's. Emily had been looking forward to showing *Judy* what a competent horsewoman she'd become.

"Well, if they don't, that's okay, too," Judy said cheerfully. "But it's going to be a lot of fun. And did you hear that Caro's going to teach Eric how to ride? She asked Matt, and he said it was okay. He said Eric could ride Andy—"

"The Appaloosa," Emily finished for her. "I suggested that to Eric this morning."

"Won't it be great if Eric really likes riding?" Judy said. "He could go with us to The Barn, and we could all ride together."

"Yeah, it would be great," Emily agreed. Judy seemed to have everything all figured out, the way she always did. Only for the past few weeks, Emily had gotten used to figuring things out for herself. She wasn't sure she liked having somebody else take charge now, not even Judy. But that was silly, she told herself sternly. Judy wasn't taking charge. She was just making a suggestion, and it was a good suggestion.

"Come on, Judy," Libby said. "You can help me saddle up Foxy. Come to think of it, you can help me groom him, too. He always rolls in the mud when he's out in the pasture overnight, and it takes me forever to clean him up. I could use a hand."

Judy grinned. "I'd love to! See you in the ring, Emily. I'm going to be watching the intermediate class to pick up some pointers." She smiled at Libby. "But I'll probably keep an eye on the advanced class, too."

Emily watched Libby and Judy go into the stables, heading for Foxy's stall. They were talking and giggling as though they'd been friends for ages, and once again Emily felt kind of funny—a little chilly, as though a cloud had passed over the brightly shining sun.

After lunch that afternoon, Emily went back to the Fillies' cabin as she had every day since she'd come to Webster's, and automatically took out her writing paper and pen. But as she sat down on her bunk, she remembered that it wasn't hers anymore, at least not while Judy was there. And since Judy was there, it would be pretty dumb to write her a letter. Emily chewed on the end of her pen, frowning. Then she brightened. She hadn't written to her grandparents for a while. Why not drop them a line?

"Hey, Emily, want to go with Penny and me to visit the mares and foals?" Dru asked, coming into the bunkhouse. "I'll show you my favorite. He's the cutest one of all, and he even lets me pet him sometimes."

"Yes, come with us, Emily," Penny added. "Libby and Lynda have gone off somewhere, and Danny's sunbathing with a couple of Thoros down by the dock. And since Judy's having her driving lesson with Chris, and Caro's teaching your brother how to ride—well, we thought . . ." She hesitated, looking at Dru.

"We thought you might be kind of lonely," Dru finished for her.

"Lonely?" Emily echoed. "Whatever gave you that idea? I like being by myself sometimes." Seeing the hurt look on Penny and Dru's faces, she added hastily, "I didn't mean I don't want company. Just let me finish writing this note to my Grandma and Grandpa, and then I'd love to come with you."

Dru and Penny brightened immediately. "Okay," Penny said. "We'll wait for you outside."

When Emily had tucked her letter into an envelope and addressed it, she and the other two girls made a detour past the mailbox in front of the farmhouse, then started off for the pasture where the Webster's mares and foals were kept. They hadn't gotten very far when they heard the clop of hooves and the squeak of buggy wheels on the road. They turned to see the buggy coming around the bend. Judy was driving, and the minute she saw them, she picked up the whip and waved it in greeting, grinning from ear to ear. Sally must have seen the whip from the corner of her eye, because she suddenly laid back her ears and began prancing around.

"Whoa, girl!" Chris shouted, grabbing the reins from Judy and pulling back. Sally rolled her eyes nervously, but calmed down at Chris's familiar touch. "Don't do that, Judy," he said. "She thought you were going to hit her or something."

"I'd *never* hit a horse," Judy told him. "I was just waving at Emily."

"Well, Sally doesn't know that. Now put the whip back into the socket."

Judy did, and Chris handed over the reins once again. "Chris let me drive all the way down to the main road and back," she said proudly to Emily, Penny, and Dru. "And I did everything right, didn't I, Chris? Until now, that is."

Emily came over and patted Sally's soft nose. She thought the little mare still looked kind of worried. "Where are you going now?" she asked Judy and Chris.

"Around the stables, then back to the main road, I guess," Chris answered.

"Then could we go down the blacktop toward Winnepac?" Judy asked eagerly. "Maybe all the way into town?"

"No way!" Chris said. "Not yet. Sally might get spooked by the cars and stuff—she's not used to traffic. And she's not really used to pulling the buggy, either. We don't drive her very much, remember."

"Whatever you say, boss," Judy said cheerfully. She slapped the reins lightly on Sally's back. "Giddyup, girl! See you later, gang," she called over her shoulder as Sally trotted off.

Penny looked wistfully after the buggy. "That sure looks like fun. I didn't even know Webster's had a buggy. I wish Chris would teach us to drive, too."

"He doesn't have time," Dru said. "Besides, Judy's special because of her broken leg, and because she's only going to be here until Sunday."

As they cut across the grass in the direction of the pasture, Penny said to Emily, "You know what I think? *I* think Chris likes Judy a lot."

Emily shrugged. "Why shouldn't he? I like her a lot, too. She's my best friend."

"I don't mean that way. I mean the way a boy likes a girl—the way your brother likes Caro."

"You're as bad as Caro is," Emily sighed. "She said the same thing, and I told her that's silly. Chris doesn't even know Judy very well."

"Emily's right, Penny," Dru said. "If Chris likes any girl, it's Emily. Remember how he gave her that pickax to go with her miner's costume at Field Day? He didn't help any of the rest of us with *our* costumes."

Emily couldn't help laughing. "Oh, yeah, right! *Every* guy gives a girl a pickax to show her he likes her!" She began to sing:

83

"I gave my love a cherry that had no stone.
I gave my love a chicken that had no bone.
I gave my love a pickax that weighed a
ton . . . "

She couldn't think of anything to rhyme with "ton," but Penny piped up, "So she can work her head off while I have fun!"

Dissolving in giggles, the three girls practically had to hold each other up.

"What's so funny?" Libby asked as she and Lynda joined Emily, Penny, and Dru. "We heard you laughing all the way down at the stable!"

"Nothing," Emily said quickly before Penny or Dru could reply. The last thing she needed was more discussion of Judy and Chris. "Just a silly song we made up. We'll sing it for you sometime. We're going to see the mares and foals. Want to come along?"

"Sure, why not?" Lynda said.

"We've been spying on Eric and Caro," Libby added, grinning as she fell into step beside Emily.

"On Eric's riding lesson," Lynda explained. "Matt's there, too—*he's* not spying, though. He's there because none of us are allowed to take our horses out without supervision, and he's giving Eric some pointers."

Glad of the change of subject, Emily asked, "How's it going?"

"Not bad. Your big brother looks real good on a horse," Libby said. "And he hasn't fallen off once. Of course, all he's done so far is walk Andy around the ring. It got pretty boring, so we left."

"Yeah, it was pretty boring, all right," Lynda said, giggling. "The last thing we heard Eric say was, 'Where's the accelerator on this thing?' I just hope he doesn't try to put Andy into reverse!"

"But you should hear Caro," Libby put in. " 'Oh, Eric, I just *knew* you were a born rider! You're so *talented*!' "

"And I bet he's eating it up," Emily said sourly.

"Like chocolate ice cream with a cherry on top," Libby told her.

"Romance sure makes people act weird," Lynda said. "Imagine Eric giving up a trip to Saratoga to stay here and do chores, just because of Caro!"

"Yeah." Emily sighed. "Eric didn't used to be interested in anything that didn't have a carburetor."

"Maybe Caro does—she has everything else," Penny said with a wide grin.

"I'm never going to have a boyfriend," Dru said solemnly. "Give me a horse any day!" She ran ahead of the others and climbed over the pasture fence. "Maybe my favorite foal will let me pet him again today."

Emily followed more slowly, wondering if Chris really did like Judy, and how Judy felt about Chris. And if Judy did like him, too, would *she* start acting weird?

Chapter Seven

"Aren't you two ready yet? They're going to start the hayride without us if you don't hurry up," Emily said to Judy and Caro that evening. The rest of the Fillies had already left for the stables, where Matt, Chris, and Eric had hitched a big wagon filled with hay to the tractor. Emily had lingered behind, hoping to have a chance to talk to Judy a little—not about anything in particular, but they hadn't had any time alone together since Judy had arrived. But Caro, as usual, took forever to get dressed. Then she decided that Judy needed some expert advice on her hair and makeup, and Judy thought that would be fun. Now Caro was putting the finishing touches on Judy's new hairstyle. She finished wrapping a multi-colored scarf around the ponytail she'd arranged on the very top of Judy's head, and stood back to admire the effect.

"*Very* cool," she said approvingly. "Here, Judy—take a look at yourself in the mirror." Caro thrust her mirror into Judy's hand, and Judy looked.

"Wow! That's neat, Caro," Judy said, grinning. "I can never do anything with my hair." She turned to Emily. "How do you like the new me?" she teased.

"It's okay," Emily said. "But I think I liked the *old* you better. With your hair sticking up like that, and all that makeup Caro put on you, you look like a stranger."

Crestfallen, Judy said, "Well, I wouldn't want to look like this all the time, but just for tonight . . . "

"You do look terrific," Emily said quickly. She hadn't meant to hurt Judy's feelings. "Now can we go?" she asked, turning to Caro.

"I guess so," Caro replied, taking one last critical glance at herself in the mirror over the bureau. "Do you think Eric will like this shirt? He's coming with us on the hayride, you know. Blue's his favorite color, and this is the bluest shirt I've got."

"It's blue, all right," Emily said, and it was. Electric blue, so bright it almost hurt her eyes. "He'll like it fine. Only if we don't get there soon, it'll be dark and he won't know what color it is!"

"Oh, Emily, don't be silly. The sun won't set for ages yet," Caro chirped.

Emily handed Judy her crutches. "Caro, it seems like wherever you go, Eric goes."

"Yes, it *does* seem that way, doesn't it?" Caro sighed happily. "I still can't get over the fact that you have such a dreamy brother."

"He's dreamy, all right," Emily muttered. "Ever since he came here, he's been like a sleepwalker. Ever since he met *you,* that is."

As they walked across the grass to the stables, Emily on one side of Judy and Caro on the other, Emily was tempted to tell Caro to cool it with Eric. She was sure Caro wouldn't have been nearly as interested in her brother if Warren were around, and she didn't want to see Eric get hurt. Caro just couldn't help flirting, though it didn't mean a thing. But before Emily could say anything, Caro started talking about how well Eric's riding lesson had gone that afternoon, and Judy began describing her driving lesson with Chris. Emily couldn't get a word in edgewise, so she plodded along in silence. Neither Caro nor Judy seemed to notice how quiet she was.

"Hey, Emily, over here!" Danny shouted as the three girls came in sight of the haywagon. "I saved you a place between Lynda and me. Hurry up!"

"Good thing the Foals aren't coming," Caro said. "We'd be packed in like sardines." She gave Eric a radiant smile and took his hand, allowing him to help her up into the wagon.

"Where are the Foals?" Judy asked Emily.

"I think they're having an old-fashioned taffy

pull with Marie in the kitchen," Emily said. "They went on the last hayride."

"Need a hand, Judy?" Chris asked, coming over to Emily and Judy. "Here, let me take those crutches. I'll stick them under the hay."

He boosted Judy up while Emily scrambled into the wagon next to Danny and Lynda. Libby, Penny, Dru, and the Thoros were already snuggled down in the hay, and Matt, seated on the tractor, called over his shoulder, "Everybody on board? Okay, let's go!"

The engine chugged, then roared, and the haywagon took off, accompanied by cheers and shouts from the campers.

"Isn't this fun?" Libby said, leaning over so Emily could hear her. "It'd be better if we had horses pulling the wagon instead of a tractor, but it's great anyway."

"Oh, yeah, it's fun, all right," Emily replied. Only it wasn't as much fun as she'd thought it would be. She'd imagined herself and Judy on the hayride, surrounded by their new friends, but Judy was sitting somewhere in the back with Chris, and Emily didn't want to intrude. If Judy, with her new hair and her new face, preferred Chris's company to hers, that was perfectly all right. So what if Judy was having a good time without her? That was what Emily had wanted, wasn't it? For Judy to have a really terrific time? And apparently Eric was having a good time, too. So Emily decided that she'd simply forget about both of them for now. She could still have fun.

Someone started singing "Found a Peanut," and everybody else raggedly joined in. Emily sang along as the sunset faded into purple, then to a deep, dark blue. Somebody else started another song. Like last night, Emily could hear Judy's voice, clear and true. She looked up into the vast dark sky sprinkled with so many stars. She never remembered seeing such a beautiful night sky when she was at home. With her head tilted back to take it all in, Emily suddenly felt very small.

"See where it looks all kind of white up there?" Danny said, interrupting her thoughts. "That's the Milky Way."

"Yeah, I know," Emily said quietly, without looking at Danny.

"I just thought I'd mention it." Danny sounded hurt.

"What's the matter with you, Emily?" Lynda finally said when Emily kept silent. "You're not in a very good mood tonight. You've hardly said a word since the hayride began."

"Yeah. I'd think you'd be happy to have your best friend and your brother here," Danny added. "*I'd* be happy if *my* best friend were here. I'm not sure about my brother, though. He can be a real pain sometimes."

"And Eric's not a pain," Lynda pointed out. "So he's dippy about Caro. So what? Mellow out, Emily."

Emily sighed. "I'm sorry," she said. "I don't mean to ruin everyone's good time. Tell me some more about the stars, Danny. I don't know any-

91

thing about them, really. But Judy does. She knows all the constellations." She leaned her head back, conscious of the prickly hay digging into her neck. "The only one I'm sure about is the Big Dipper."

Danny smiled. "Well, that's the Little Dipper," she said, pointing, "and over there's Orion, the hunter. His belt is clear as anything tonight. And then there's . . . "

Emily tuned Danny out. She was really listening to the voices and laughter coming from the back of the wagon, where Libby had joined Judy and Chris. She could hear Dru and Penny's voices, too, and Eric saying, "Next year I'll get my license, and then I'll be able to drive. I've been doing part-time jobs, and I'm saving all my money so I'll be able to buy a car—maybe a Camaro."

Caro said, "Camaros are really cool. I bet you're going to be a terrific driver. I mean, you're so well-coordinated and all."

"*Chris!*" Judy squealed. "Don't stuff hay down my back! It tickles!"

"That wasn't me—it was Libby! Libby, cut that out!"

"Who, me? It was an accident. I was aiming for Penny, but Judy got in the way."

Emily heard lots of giggles, then a screech that definitely came from Caro.

"*Libby!* I'll get you for that!"

"Hay fight! Hay fight!" one of the Thoros yelled happily.

92

"*Eric!* They're getting hay all over my hair! Make them stop!"

"Take it easy. Judy got hay up my nose."

"Serves you right! Just because my leg's in a cast doesn't mean I'm an invalid! *Whoops!* Sorry, Dru."

"*Achoo!* Hay always makes me sneeze."

And then, close to her ear, Emily heard " . . . and see over there? That's Cassiopeia's Chair, with all those little stars . . . Emily? Are you okay?"

"Yeah, I'm fine, Danny. Everything's just fine."

But everything wasn't just fine. Emily snuggled down deeper into the hay and stared up at the stars. If everyone else was having such a good time, why wasn't she? The hay was making her itch—she could feel wisps of it sticking into her neck. And she was chilly, too. Why hadn't she thought to bring a sweatshirt or something?

"Let's sing another song," Judy called out. "Emily, what would you like to sing?"

"I don't care," Emily called back. She didn't feel like singing. Her throat felt all tight and scratchy. *Maybe I'm coming down with a cold*, she thought. Some fun this hayride was turning out to be!

"How about 'You Are My Sunshine'?" she heard someone say. Judy started the song, and the others joined in. Judy was having fun, all right, and so were all the rest of the Fillies and Thoros. Eric was probably enjoying himself with Caro. Emily couldn't help feeling left out. This wasn't the way she'd pictured herself and Judy spending her best friend's brief visit to Webster's.

"Come on, Emily. Sing!" Lynda playfully poked her in the ribs, but Emily shook her head, so Lynda and Danny left her alone, singing at the top of their lungs.

Emily could hardly wait for the hayride to be over.

"Emily, wait up!" Judy called, hobbling up on her crutches. Everyone had just finished sampling the taffy the Foals had made, and the Fillies and Thoros were heading back to their cabins.

Emily waited, and Judy caught up to her. "Is something wrong?" she asked. "You were awfully quiet tonight."

Emily looked at her best friend's usually cheerful face, solemn now in the moonlight, and suddenly decided that she'd tell Judy exactly what was on her mind. They always told each other everything, or at least they used to. They'd known each other for ten of their thirteen years, and they'd never kept secrets from one another.

"Kind of," Emily said. "Something's been bothering me, and maybe it's silly, but . . . "

"Hey, Judy, let's tell ghost stories tonight after lights out," Libby said, bounding up to them. "I know some good scary ones. Unless you're tired, that is."

"No, I'm not tired," Judy said with a grin. "I know some scary ones, too. Remember the one about the guy whose hair turned white overnight

94

after he saw—" She glanced briefly at Libby. "Remember what he saw in the haunted house, Emily?"

"Yeah, I remember," Emily said with a sigh. "You tell that one really well. You're a much better storyteller than I am."

"Great!" Libby cried. "You go first, Judy, as soon as we're all in bed and the lights are out. This is gonna be fun!"

Judy turned to Emily. "You said something was bothering you. What is it?"

Emily shook her head. "Never mind. It can wait. I guess it wasn't really very important anyway."

"We'll talk about it tomorrow, okay?"

"Okay," Emily said softly. "Tomorrow."

Chapter Eight

Even before Emily opened her eyes the next morning, she knew it was raining. She could hear the steady drumming of rain on the roof directly over her head, and as she rolled onto her back, a drop of water hit her right on the tip of her nose.

"Rats!" she muttered, squinting up at the ceiling where another drop hung suspended, ready to fall. She moved out of the way and sighed. Terrific. Just what she needed. A rainy day and a leaky roof. Well, at least her sore throat had gone away. That was one thing to be thankful for, anyway.

She leaned over the edge of her bunk and looked around the cabin. As usual, she was the first one awake. Judy, Pam, and the Fillies were still sound asleep. From directly underneath her, Emily heard steady, rhythmical snoring. *What do you know! Caro snores!* she thought. Maybe she ought to tell Eric. But why bother? He'd probably think it was cute.

Because of the rain, Emily couldn't pay her morning visit to Joker. And because of the rain, riding classes would have to be held in the indoor ring, which meant that the three groups would either have to take turns, or they'd all have one big class together. And because of the rain, Judy wouldn't be able to have a driving lesson today, which was too bad since she only had three more days at Webster's.

I do want her to have a good time, Emily said to herself. And Judy had certainly enjoyed the storytelling last night. She'd had all the Fillies shivering with delicious terror as she told story after story about haunted houses and phantom stagecoaches. And they had all shrieked with laughter when she told the one about the lady who always wore a black ribbon around her neck until one day somebody untied it and her head fell off. Yes, Judy was popular, all right. If anybody took a vote on the most popular camper at Webster's, Judy would probably win by a landslide.

Emily wriggled out of the way just in time to avoid another drip from the leaky roof. Then she had a happy thought. Because of the rain, maybe she and Judy would have time for a nice, quiet talk, since Emily wouldn't be riding all day. Now that she thought about it, Emily was glad she hadn't told Judy how neglected she'd felt last night. After all, it wasn't Judy's fault that all Emily's friends were making such a fuss about

97

her. Judy was just a really nice, really fun person. That was why she was Emily's best friend.

Emily wanted to talk to someone about Caro and Eric, and Judy was a good listener. But come to think of it, Judy had said the other day that she didn't think Caro was as bad as Emily had made her out to be. On the other hand, Eric wasn't Judy's big brother, so she didn't care as much as Emily did that he was acting like a dope, or that he'd be miserable when he went back home and wrote letters that Caro didn't answer. Well, Emily would explain, and Judy would understand, and then Emily would feel much better.

Wasn't anybody ever going to wake up?

In spite of the rain, or maybe because of it, things didn't work out the way Emily had planned. At breakfast, Matt announced that the beginners would have their class first in the indoor ring while the intermediate and advanced riders mucked out their horses' stalls and cleaned their saddles and bridles with saddle soap and neat's-foot oil. Then it would be the intermediates' turn in the ring, and after lunch, the advanced riders would have their class. After that, everyone would gather in the farmhouse to watch a new video the Websters had just received of the equestrian competitions in the last Olympics. And after that . . .

Matt went on and on, outlining the day's activities. It seemed to Emily that there was more to do on a rainy day at Webster's than when it was sunny.

"Want to help me groom Joker?" she asked Judy as they pulled the hoods of their waterproof ponchos over their heads before stepping out into the rain. "He's going to be covered with mud after spending the night out in the pasture."

"Gee, I'd like to, Emily," Judy said, "but Dru asked me to help her clean up Donna, and I said I would. She's still not quite sure about everything she's supposed to do. If I have time, I'll help you with Joker, okay? Maybe after the beginners' class starts."

"Sure, whenever you have time," Emily said. "I don't really need any help. I just thought you might not have anything to do."

"Oh, I have lots to do," Judy said happily. "Don't worry about me."

"You ready, Judy?" Dru asked, coming out of the house in her bright yellow slicker. "I don't want to rush you or anything, but since my class is first, I want to get started on Donna right away, 'cause she's gonna be *filthy*. I have an apple for her in my pocket. Donna loves apples."

"I have one for Sally, too," Judy said. "Come on, let's go!"

"Can you manage those crutches all right in the rain?" Emily asked.

Judy grinned. "By now, I think I could probably get through a snowdrift on the darned things!" She swung herself expertly down the porch steps, calling over her shoulder, "See you later, Emily."

"Yeah, see you later."

"Judy's something else, isn't she?" Danny said

99

admiringly as she came over to stand next to Emily on the porch. "Nothing gets her down. If I'd broken my leg and had to sit around most of the summer instead of coming to Webster's, I'd probably be feeling so sorry for myself that nobody would want to have anything to do with me!"

"She's something else, all right," Emily agreed.

The two girls started off for the stables side by side in the pouring rain. Suddenly Libby darted past them shouting, "Hey, Judy, wait up!"

"You know, Judy's a lot like Libby," Danny said. "They're both bouncy and bubbly and full of fun. I guess that's why they hit it off so well."

"And I'm not," Emily mumbled as she splashed through a puddle.

"Not what?"

"Bouncy and bubbly and full of fun."

"Yes, you are," Danny said, then added, "or you are most of the time, anyway. You sure you're feeling all right?"

"I'm fine," Emily said. Her right foot was soaking wet—there must be a hole in the sole of her boot.

A group of giggling Thoros, along with Caro, Lynda, and Penny, came sloshing along, singing "Singing in the Rain." Danny started whistling the tune, but Emily didn't join in.

"Caro, will you please stop singing that dumb song?" Emily sighed a little while later. She was scrubbing the mud off Joker's white socks, using

101

a soft-bristled brush and a pail of warm water, and Caro, in Vic's stall next door, was busy grooming the big bay. She hadn't stopped singing since they'd come into the stable, and it was driving Emily crazy.

Caro broke off in the middle of a bar. "Sorry," she said cheerfully. "I didn't know I was bothering you."

"Well, you were." Emily finished Joker's left hind leg and moved behind him to his other side, patting him gently on the rump so he wouldn't be startled.

"Hey, Emily, notice anything different about me?" Caro asked. She had come over to the partition dividing the two stalls, and now she folded her arms on top of it.

"No," Emily said. She didn't look up. She hadn't paid much attention to Caro in the bunkhouse or at breakfast, but she certainly hadn't seen anything unusual about the pretty blond girl.

"*Look* at me," Caro urged, so Emily did. "Notice anything now?"

Emily looked closely. Come to think of it, Caro *did* look different, but she couldn't quite figure out why.

Caro grinned. "I'm not wearing any makeup! Well, hardly any—just a little mascara and eye liner. If I don't use anything at all, I look like a white rabbit . . . or a light bulb!"

Emily was amazed. She'd never before heard Caro admit to being less than perfect. "Eric told me last night he doesn't like to see a lot of makeup on a girl," Caro went on. "He likes the natural look. I *do* look natural, don't I?" she asked anxiously.

So that was it. *I might have known,* Emily thought. *Eric again.* "Yeah, very natural," she said, and went back to Joker's right hind leg.

"Good! I thought I did." Caro kept standing there while Emily scrubbed. Mingled with the sounds of the other campers' voices and the occasional snort or stamping of their mounts, Emily could hear the pounding of hammers on the upper level of the stable, which meant that Eric and Chris were hard at work. "Emily?"

Emily frowned. "What now?"

"You're still mad at me because I tried to take Joker away from you, aren't you?" Caro asked.

"Don't be silly! That was weeks ago." Emily polished Joker's hoof vigorously.

"I know. I'm really sorry I did that. I like Vic a lot now. We're getting along just fine."

"Good."

"Well, if you're not mad at me because of Joker, then why *are* you mad at me?" Caro asked.

"Caro, I am *not* mad at you! But Vic will be if you don't get all that mud off him," Emily said. "And so will Matt."

"It's your brother, isn't it?" Caro continued. "You think I'm just playing games with Eric. You don't believe I really care about him, do you?" Caro's voice was so low that nobody but Emily could hear her, and when Emily looked up, she saw that Caro's face was flushed, and her big,

103

beautiful eyes were filled with tears. This was a Caro Emily had never seen before.

Emily didn't know what to say. Everything Caro had just said was absolutely true, but hearing it made Emily feel ashamed of herself for some reason. She sat back on her heels in the straw, pretending to be absorbed in washing out her brush while Caro kept on looking at her, waiting for her answer.

Finally, she admitted, "That's about it, I guess."

"Well, it's not true!" Caro said hotly. "I *do* care about him. He's the nicest boy I ever met!"

"Caro, *every* boy's the nicest boy you ever met," Emily said irritably. "First it was Warren, and then the boys from Long Branch, and now it's Eric." She looked Caro straight in the eye. "I don't care what you say. I just don't like watching you make a fool of my brother, and that's exactly what you're doing. You'd drop him like a hot potato if somebody more interesting came along; somebody rich like you. And when Eric goes back home, you'll forget all about him."

Instead of making some nasty comment and turning her back as Emily expected her to do, Caro slowly shook her head. "You're wrong, Emily, about a lot of things. I'm not really boy crazy like everybody thinks, and I *do* care about Eric. And the other thing is—"

"Hey, you two, what's up?" Pam stopped by Joker's stall and peered inside. "Boy, those are a couple of really dirty horses! Haven't you started grooming them yet? Emily, you'd better get on with it. The beginners' class is about to start, and your class is next." She patted both horses' noses, then strode briskly off in the direction of the tack room.

"I was about to tell you something important," Caro said when Pam was out of earshot. "Don't you want to know what it is?"

Emily wasn't sure if she did or not, but Caro looked so serious that she couldn't help feeling curious. "Okay, what is it?" she asked.

Caro took a deep breath. "You said I'd drop Eric the minute I met somebody rich like me. Well, I'm *not* rich. My folks probably aren't any richer than yours. And they're not spending the summer in Europe. My mom's working in my dad's real estate office until school starts. She's a teacher at Spencer Academy, the private school I go to. I get free tuition, or else Mother and Daddy wouldn't be able to afford to send me there. And the reason I came to Webster's instead of some big, expensive horse camp is because we can't afford that, either."

Emily stared at her, open-mouthed. "But all those things you said—all your clothes . . ." Then her eyes narrowed. "You're putting me on, aren't you? You're making this up."

"Oh, for Pete's sake, Emily!" Caro snapped, sounding more like her old self. "Why would I do a thing like that?" She sighed, and her shoulders slumped. "I wanted everybody to *think* I was rich. *That's* what I made up! Some of my clothes are

105

things I saved my money to buy. But most of them are hand-me-downs from my cousins. They have all the money."

"But why—" Emily began, then caught sight of Pam returning, a bridle slung over her shoulder. "Quick! Get busy!" she hissed, picking up a curry-comb and beginning to rub Joker's mud-encrusted coat. Caro began vigorously brushing Vic. When Pam had passed, Emily said, "Then why are you so snobby all the time?"

"Because that's the way most of the girls at my school act," Caro said. "They used to make my life miserable when I was so fat. . . ."

"*Fat?*" Emily echoed, astonished. "You were *fat?*"

"As fat as a pig," Caro told her, "until this past year, when Mother and Daddy sent me to a really good doctor who specializes in weight control. I lost a lot of weight between last September and this June. But when I started getting slimmer, the other girls still didn't like me any better. The boys did, though. I guess that's why I like flirting so much—I still can't quite believe I'm pretty!"

Emily leaned against Joker, unable to believe what she was hearing. All she could say was, "Wow!"

Caro kept on brushing Vic. She didn't look at Emily. "When I came here," she said, "I figured nobody knew anything about me, so I could be anybody I wanted to be. For once, I could be in charge. I was going to have the best of everything, instead of always being pushed around. And then things kind of snowballed, you know what I mean?" Now she met Emily's eyes. "I wanted to make friends with all you guys, only . . . well, it was like I was trapped inside this person I made up, and I couldn't get out. And now the summer's more than half over, and it's too late."

"Maybe not," Emily said softly. "We always wanted to be your friends, Caro. We still do, if you'll let us. And as for my brother . . . " She smiled. "I guess that's between you and Eric. I shouldn't have butted in."

Caro's face lit up, and Emily thought how much prettier she was without all that makeup. "Matt said I could give him another riding lesson after lunch," she said. "He really *is* going to be a good rider, once he gets the hang of it."

Joker, who had been standing patiently all this time, now turned his head and nudged Emily with his nose, whuffling gently.

"Oh, Joker," Emily sighed, putting her arms around his neck and giving him a big hug. "I'm sorry! I've been neglecting you, and I didn't mean to. Don't worry. I'll polish you till you shine like the sun."

"It'll be the only sun we're likely to see today!" Caro said, giggling. She went back to grooming Vic, and as she worked, she started singing again. But this time, Emily didn't mind. She was too stunned by what Caro had just told her. Imagine! Caro had been fat and unhappy, just like Dru! And she was a completely different person than she had seemed to be. That would take some getting used to!

Chapter Nine

Emily couldn't wait to tell Judy everything Caro had said, but somehow there just wasn't time. Emily had barely finished grooming Joker and cleaning out his stall when it was time for her riding class. After lunch, during rest period, Penny and Dru challenged Judy to a game of Monopoly, and Emily had to go back to the stable and clean Joker's tack. Then Libby, Lynda, and Caro asked Judy to watch the advanced riding class, and after that was the video, then chores, and supper, and games in the activity room. Whatever was going on, Judy was always busy, and so was Emily. Judy didn't seem to be making any effort to seek Emily out. It was weird—when Judy was back home and Emily was writing to her every day, she'd been able to share everything with her friend. But now that Judy was here, they weren't sharing anything at all.

Saturday dawned bright and clear, as though the whole world had been washed by yesterday's rain. After Emily had paid her morning visit to Joker, she felt as if all the cobwebs had been washed out of her brain as well. This would be Judy's last full day at Webster's, since Emily's parents would be arriving on Sunday to pick up Judy and Eric and take them home. So today she'd have to find a way to spend some time alone with Judy. It was really ridiculous that they hadn't been able to get together until now. She was sure that Judy must feel the same way. After all, they'd been best friends for most of their lives!

But it wasn't until rest period after lunch that Emily finally had her opportunity. Though Caro had asked her to come and watch Eric's riding lesson, Emily refused, saying that she was sure it would not make her brother very happy to have his little sister keeping an eye on him. Before Libby or any of the other Fillies could ask Judy to do anything with them, Emily took her aside.

"Come on, Judy," she said. "Let's take a walk down by the river. I have so much to tell you that I think I'll explode if we don't have a chance to talk!"

"Great!" Judy said. "But I have a better idea. Chris said he'd let me drive Sally all by myself today, so why don't you come along? I can't wait to show you how much I've learned!"

"That's okay with me, if Chris doesn't mind," Emily said.

"If Chris doesn't mind what?" Chris came up next to them, and fell into step beside the girls as they headed for the stables.

Before Emily could answer, Judy said, "I've asked Emily to take a buggy ride with me. That's all right with you, isn't it?"

"Well . . ." Chris frowned. "I guess it'll be okay, as long as you keep your mind on your driving and don't try any funny stuff."

"Funny stuff?" Judy repeated innocently. "I don't know what you mean. I'm not going to race poor old Sally or anything. We'll just go down the dirt road and back, the way I did with you."

"All right. But just remember, Sally's easily spooked. She may be old, but she's feisty, and like I told you, she really hates cars. Don't go all the way down to the Winnepac road, 'cause if she bolts, you're not going to be able to control her."

"I bet I could," Judy said. "You told me yourself what a good driver I am. C'mon, Emily, I'll show you how to hitch Sally to the buggy. I can do that even with my leg in a cast!"

A few minutes later, Judy was in the driver's position holding Sally's reins, and Emily climbed up beside her on the seat.

"We're off!" Judy cried. She clucked to the little mare, and Sally broke into a brisk trot.

Emily was a little tense at first, but Judy seemed to know what she was doing, so she began to relax.

110

"Isn't this fun?" Judy said. "Not as much fun as actually riding, but it's fun anyway. So what did you want to tell me about?"

Emily started telling her everything Caro had said the previous morning, but she got the impression that Judy wasn't really listening. And the minute she stopped talking, Judy said, "Driving's really very much like riding, you know. You have to feel the horse's mouth through the reins, and you mustn't pull too hard, or the horse gets confused about the signals you're sending. Sally has a very tender mouth. Hey, Emily, when we come back, will you take a picture of Sally and me? I kind of feel like she's *my* horse, the way Joker's yours."

"Sure," Emily said. She glanced over at Judy. "Did you hear anything I just said?"

"Of course I did. You said Caro's not really rich so it's okay that Eric likes her. Whoa, Sally. Slow down! I told Chris I wouldn't race you. Are you going to make a liar out of me?"

Emily looked down the dirt road. In the distance she could see the mailman's blue-and-white truck coming toward them. "Judy, watch out for that truck," she said.

"Truck? What truck? Oh, *that* truck. No problem. It's coming real slow. Sally's not going to care about—*Sally*! Now cut that out!" Judy pulled back on the reins, but the little mare was dancing around between the shafts, tossing her head nervously.

"Maybe we'd better turn around," Emily suggested.

"Don't be such a scaredy-cat, Emily," Judy said, sawing on the reins. She managed to slow Sally to a fidgety walk, but just as they came abreast of the truck, it backfired, and Sally reared, took the bit in her teeth, and plunged forward. Emily grabbed onto the buggy seat with both hands, then let go and seized Judy's arm to prevent her from toppling to the ground.

"Let go!" Judy yelled. "I can handle it! Let me do it by myself!"

Sally streaked past the mail truck, the buggy bouncing and lurching in her wake, and Emily hung on for dear life both to Judy and the seat. Judy dropped one of the reins, and Emily let go of her arm to pick it up.

"*Pull*!" she shouted. "You pull on your rein and I'll pull on mine! Don't panic. It'll be okay!"

Judy pulled with all her might, and so did Emily. Between them, they managed to slow Sally down from a gallop to a canter to a walk, and finally to a stop. Emily leaped out of the buggy and ran around to Sally's head, stroking the terrified mare and whispering, "There, there. It's okay, Sally. Don't be scared. Everything's all right." But she was so scared herself that she could hardly get the words out.

"Emily?" Judy's voice was barely audible. She was as frightened as Emily and Sally were.

"I'm still here," Emily said shakily. "And so's Sally. Are you all right?"

"I—I think so . . . . " Judy suddenly burst into tears.

For a moment, Emily just stared at her. The last time she'd seen Judy cry was when they were both seven years old and Judy's puppy had been hit by a car. Since Sally seemed to have recovered enough to start munching on some of the weeds growing by the side of the road, Emily scrambled back into the buggy and touched her friend gently on the shoulder.

"Are you okay?" she asked. "You're not hurt, are you?"

"N-n-no," Judy stammered between sobs.

"Then what's wrong?"

"*Everything!*" Judy wailed.

Emily put her arm around her. "What do you mean, everything?"

"Oh, just *everything*! You, and me, and Webster's, and this whole awful summer." Judy bent over and buried her face in her folded arms.

"Maybe I'd better tie Sally to the fence, and then we'll talk," Emily said softly.

When she returned, Judy had dried her eyes and was wiping her runny nose on her sleeve. "Got a tissue?" she croaked.

"No. But you can use my bandanna," Emily said, pulling a blue-and-white cotton kerchief out of her hip pocket. "Here, blow."

Judy blew. "I couldn't wait to come here with your family," she mumbled. "Even though I was only going to be here for a few days, I thought it would be so great. I mean, you and me, the way we'd planned for so long. But it was all . . ." she gulped for breath, " . . . *different. You're* different. It's like I don't know you anymore!"

Emily frowned. "Different? What do you mean?"

"Oh, I don't know. Or maybe I do. You've made so many new friends. Every time I wanted to talk to you, just the two of us, there were all these other people around. Libby, and Lynda, and Penny, and Dru, and Danny, and even Caro." Judy blew her nose again. "And you're such a good rider—you're *miles* ahead of me! That's why I wanted to learn to drive—so there was something I could do that you couldn't! But I'm not even good at that."

Emily realized that her mouth was hanging open and she immediately closed it. "But Judy," she said, "that's exactly the way I've been feeling about *you!*" She met Judy's astonished gaze. "When you got here, I was so happy I didn't know what to do. And then you just seemed to take over, and I felt left out in the cold. All of a sudden, my friends were *your* friends. And they all liked you much better than me. I started getting really mad at you because I thought you were doing it on purpose. I hated myself for feeling that way, but I couldn't help it."

"Oh, wow!" Judy whispered. "Boy, were we a couple of nut cases!"

"I guess we were," Emily said. "But we're not anymore, are we?"

"No, we're not." Judy gave her a teary smile. "We're still best friends, right?"

"Better believe it!" Emily beamed. Then she had another thought. "Uh . . . Judy, how do you feel about Chris?"

"Chris? You mean, do I feel about him the way Caro feels about Eric?"

Emily nodded.

Judy giggled. "No way! He's just a lot of fun. Why?"

Emily thought about that for a minute. "I like Chris a lot, too, but just as a friend who happens to be a boy, not as a boyfriend. Besides, horses are a lot more interesting than boys!" she added with a grin.

"They sure are!" Judy blew her nose one last time, then handed the bandanna back to Emily.

Emily glanced at Sally, who was placidly nibbling the fresh, sweet grass by the road. She didn't even flinch when the mail truck made its return trip right past her. "Speaking of Chris," Emily said, "if we don't get back to the stable soon, he's going to send a search team after us!"

Judy looked at her shyly. "You won't tell him that I couldn't handle Sally when she freaked out over that mail truck, will you?"

Emily blinked her eyes. "Mail truck? What mail truck?" She jumped down and untied Sally from the fence, then hopped back up on the seat next to Judy. Grinning, she said, "Home, James!"

* * *

116

"I really enjoyed that fancy riding exhibition," Emily's father said on Sunday afternoon. "What do you call it again? Dressing, or something like that?"

"*Dressage,* Daddy," Emily told him, squeezing his arm affectionately as they walked to the Jordans' car. Eric had already stowed Judy's wheelchair (which she hadn't used once) in the trunk, and he was holding Caro's hand while she gazed at him adoringly. Emily caught Judy's glance and they both rolled their eyes. Behind Eric's back, Judy puckered her lips, pantomiming an exaggerated kiss, and Emily nearly burst out laughing.

"That was very impressive," Mrs. Jordan said, "but what impressed me even more was to see how well Eric has learned to ride in the past few days." She beamed at her son, and Eric blushed.

"Aw, Mom, I'm not very good at all compared to Caro—or even Emily," he added. "Now those people who rode in the exhibition were something else. It must take *years* to learn to make a horse dance like that, and one of the riders was only a little kid. I'm still just finding out which end of a horse is which."

"The most important thing to remember," Judy said solemnly, "is that you put the fuel in the *front* end of a horse, not the back, like a car."

"You're so sharp, it's a wonder you don't cut yourself," Eric said, aiming a playful punch at her, but Judy hobbled out of the way and made a face at him.

"You're absolutely right, Mrs. Jordan," Caro

said. "I've never seen anybody learn all the basics of riding so fast." She squeezed Eric's hand. "I bet when you come with your folks to pick Emily up at the end of the season, you'll be even better—if you ride at that stable you told me about while you're home."

"Are you going to start riding at The Barn, Eric?" Emily asked, surprised. "It's expensive, you know. I thought you were saving up for that Camaro."

"Uh . . . well, yeah, I am, but . . . well, I thought they might let me help out around the place the way you and Judy used to do, and then maybe they'd give me a reduced rate."

Judy said sweetly, "Emily and I would be more than happy to give you a recommendation, wouldn't we, Emily?"

"Oh, yes," Emily said, equally sweetly. "And maybe they'd even let you ride Frosty."

"Gee, do you think Eric will be able to handle him?" Judy asked with mock concern.

Emily could hardly keep a straight face as she said, "Oh, I think he probably could." She and Judy both knew that Frosty, the horse Judy usually rode at The Barn back home, was as slow as molasses in January, and seemed to plod over the trails in his sleep.

"Well, gang, I think it's time to hit the road," Mr. Jordan said. "We have a long drive ahead of us." He gave Emily a big hug. "Honey, I'm really proud of you. Take care of yourself, and keep us posted on what you and your friends are doing."

119

"I will, Daddy. Drive carefully. And I don't think you'll have to wait to hear from me about what's going on at Webster's," Emily whispered in his ear. "I have a feeling Eric's going to be getting a lot of mail!"

"You know, I believe you're right," her father said with a wink.

Emily gave her mother a kiss and a hug, then turned to Judy. The two girls threw their arms around each other. "I'm so glad you came!" Emily said. "Give my love to your folks. And I'll keep writing every day—well, *almost* every day."

"You'd better, or I'll never speak to you again," Judy told her. "And, Emily . . . I'm awfully glad we're friends."

Emily grinned. "Me, too!"

Judy got into the car, and Emily handed her crutches in after her.

"Eric, time to go," Mr. Jordan called, sticking his head out the car window. "And this time we can't leave you behind."

"Coming, Dad." Eric looked down at Caro. They were still holding hands. "Well . . . nice meeting you, Caro," he mumbled. "You'll write to me, won't you?"

"Of course! And you'll write back, won't you?" Caro asked softly.

"I sure will. I'll be seeing you in a couple of weeks, when we come to pick up Emily."

"I can hardly wait," Caro breathed.

"Eric!" Now Mrs. Jordan stuck her head out the window as Mr. Jordan gunned the engine.

"Coming," Eric said, finally dropping Caro's hand. He was about to get into the car, when Emily tapped him on the shoulder.

"Aren't you forgetting something?" she asked, grinning.

"Huh? Oh, yeah. Bye, Emily." He got in and slammed the door.

"Brothers!" Emily said with an exasperated sigh.

She and Caro waved until the Jordans' car disappeared beyond a bend in the road. As they started across the grass toward the Fillies' cabin, Caro said dreamily, "I think I'll write a letter to Eric right now."

"Oh, no, you won't," Emily told her. "The Fillies are on garden detail, remember? We have to pick the vegetables for supper tonight. Everybody else is already working."

Caro pouted prettily. "*Really*, Emily," she said with a trace of the old Caro whine, "I think I'm coming down with one of my headaches. . . . "

"Baloney!" Emily said cheerfully. "No more 'privileged princess' act, Caro. You know Eric wouldn't like it."

The pout vanished immediately. "You're right, he wouldn't like it one bit." Suddenly she grinned. "Race you to the vegetable patch!" She dashed off, her blond ponytail streaming behind her.

As Emily sprinted after her, she decided that

the "new, improved" Caro wasn't hard to take at all.

"Hey, Caro, no fair!" she shouted. "You got a head start. Wait for me!"

Why is a suspicious-looking stranger poking around Webster's Country Horse Camp? Emily, Libby, and the other Fillies are sure that the camp is going to be sold, and they set out to stop it. Their crazy plans include skunks—and worse! Will the Fillies be able to save the camp? Or will this be their last summer at Webster's?

Don't miss HORSE CRAZY #5
Horse Play by Virginia Vail

ABOUT THE AUTHOR

Virginia Vail is a pseudonym of the author of over a dozen young adult novels, most recently the ANIMAL INN series. She is the mother of two grown children, both of whom are animal lovers, and lives in Forest Hills, New York with one fat gray cat. Many years ago, Virginia Vail fell in love with a beautiful palomino named Joker. She always wanted to put him in a book. Now she has.